WE RUN
OVER SNAKES

WE RUN OVER SNAKES

A fictional novel in a true
historic setting and time

Barbara (Tolman) Schrodt

Author Reputation Press LLC
45 Dan Road Suite 5
Canton MA 02021
www.authorreputationpress.com
Hotline: 1(888) 821-0229
Fax: 1(508) 545-7580

Ordering Information:
Quantity sales. Special discounts are available on quantity purchases by corporations, associations, and others. For details, contact the publisher at the address above.

Printed in the United States of America.

ISBN-13:	Softcover	978-1-64961-904-4
	eBook	978-1-64961-876-4

Library of Congress Control Number: 2021919615

Many individuals have believed in the worthiness of this work, and have contributed in various ways to getting this story told. They include Mrs. Halene Pince, an actual homesteader's wife and the author's high school typing teacher.

But, more than anyone, this author must tearfully thank her old neighbors and friends, Gordon and Ina Mae Harris. Gordon was one of the original Third Division homesteaders. Without Gordon's input on the farming components of this book, this story could never have been told.

Gordon Harris is a humble man, but this opportunity must be taken to thank him for being the Representative to the Riverton Farm Unit Adjustment Committee that worked with the United States Bureau of Reclamation and Government. He was selected as the Representative for North Pavillion, Wyoming, while among the youngest of the homesteaders and yet single. He put in much diligent, sincere effort and time in representing so many families as he helped pass the law PL 258, among other notable achievements.

Mr. Harris also started a 4H group called "Hard-at-Work" which won recognition across the state with some of the 4H projects of the Third Division children. He and his wife sacrificed valuable time from their farm to accompany homesteader's youngsters to 4H camp during the summers. Gordon doesn't know it, but this author's ability and confidence to professionally address groups that sometimes include hundreds of people, came from Gordon's mandates that each 4H member stand and give a short talk.

Contents

Chapter 1 From Here To There 1

Chapter 2 Through the Eyes of a Child 15

Chapter 3 A Bright Spot 23

Chapter 4 A Team... 32

Chapter 5 A Man's Work... 35

Chapter 6 Priorities... 40

Chapter 7 A Letter from the Sticks.......................... 45

Chapter 8 Friends Become Family 47

Chapter 9 A Homestead Christmas.......................... 51

Chapter 10 Is It Really Spring?................................. 62

Chapter 11 Faith Versus Fear................................... 66

Chapter 12 Frills... 72

Chapter 13 Settling Things....................................... 77

Chapter 14 Womenfolk 98

Chapter 15 "But, They Smell." 107

Chapter 16 Faltering Harvest................................... 113

Chapter 17 High Water Table................................... 118

Chapter 18 What Now?.. 126

Chapter 19 The Dread Polio 135

Chapter 20 Harsh Realities...................................... 152

Chapter 21 A Wyoming Blizzard.............................. 156

Chapter 22 The Leperous Land................................ 167

Chapter 23   A Breath Of City 170

Chapter 24   What's His Plan? 177

Chapter 25   Bad Breath 182

Chapter 26   Public Law 258 187

Chapter 27   Beloved Traitorous Soil 190

Chapter 28   Rattled 195

Chapter 29   A Rescue Is Planned 201

Chapter 30   The Mastery of the Land 207

Chapter 31   A Date to Remember 213

Chapter 32   Mountains Beckon 230

Chapter 33   This Side of the Battle 238

Chapter 34   New Tensions 245

Chapter 35   The 'Option' 251

Chapter 36 260

Dedicated to my fine parents,

Gene and Alice Tolman,

homesteaders of this

Third Division.

Their ethics of honesty,

faith, and hard work

made them conquerors in

my eyes, regardless of

the land.

CHAPTER 1

From Here To There

The Elwoods

IT WAS THERE! The envelope was third in the pile of mail drawn from the old bent metal mailbox. Charlotte's heart sped up with excitement and fear. Her blue eyes were shiny with tears, her blond hair sticking out like straw from underneath her bandanna.

"John! John! It's here. We got it. That letter's here!" Charlotte's voice shouted over the sound of her unevenly worn leather shoes hitting the dirt lane as she raced towards the barn.

John's face appeared around the barn door casing, its expression wide with hope and expectation. "What does it say?"

John's grin stretched his weather-roughened face, making his cheekbones even more pronounced. Charlotte loved the way his brown eyes danced when excited. The two reached in practiced rhythm to pull out two cream cans to sit upon, side by side. John straddled his, while Charlotte perched more on the edge.

The Jersey cow stomped her foot and swished her tail at a bothersome fly, turning her head in the stanchion to fling saliva across her shoulder. She seemed surprised that the milking had stopped after only two teats had been emptied. John reached back and pulled the foaming milk bucket farther from the cow's restless foot.

"Read it, Charlotte. We might as well know what it says. We'll live with it either way." John's brown eyes peered intently into Charlotte's vulnerable-looking blue ones. John trusted his reading abilities less than he did his wife's. She had finished high school, but he had dropped out of junior high to work at the factory when his father had lost his job in the Depression.

With an indrawn breath, Charlotte tapped the end of the white business-sized envelope, ripped off the tiniest ribbon of the end, and blew the envelope open. With trembling fingers, she pulled out the folded sheets.

Her silent prayer was imperceptible. *Dear God, don't let this break his heart.* She began to read carefully aloud.

"Dear Mr. Elwood, this letter comes to you after careful evaluation of the documents you provided. Your financial statement, your honorable discharge from the military, your references, plus your outlined goals have met the requirements as presented." Charlotte glanced up at the piercing eyes and trembling lips on her husband's handsome face. She drew a breath, licked her lips, and continued.

"Therefore, please find enclosed a map of the Wyoming, Fremont County Third Division Irrigation Project. You will see that there are 87 available homestead plats, each measuring approximately 160 acres."

"John! Look here! There's a map. Oh, Honey, it's really going to happen!" Charlotte's words were finished in John's arms as he leaped up and wrapped his strong sun-tanned arms around her and spun Charlotte in the air. His laughter was mingled with something like a yelp.

Giggling and wiping away her tears, Charlotte settled herself back on her cream can and continued reading while her husband paced.

"The homestead plats are marked. Please return the enclosed form 'Application for Plat' with your number one choice of properties, along with your number two choice. This application must be received by August 1, 1949, in order to be included in the drawing. While each candidate's first choice will be considered, each plat will be awarded in the most fair method available. Each candidate will receive only one plat.

"If, when you receive notice of the plat awarded to you, you are displeased with that particular parcel of ground, you may drop out of the drawing. An alternate list of applicants awaits the opportunity to accept your plat if you relinquish it. There may be other homesteads offered in the future, although none are planned at this time, in this Wyoming area or any other. You may expect to receive notice of the plat you've been assigned by November 30, 1949. Please prepare to complete all agreed-upon improvements to the land within three years from date you receive notice of your identified plat."

Raising her head to smile at her husband, Charlotte discovered tears trailing down his weathered cheeks, matching her own. She rose and carefully held the letter over his shoulder in one hand as they shared a gentle kiss.

Taking the map from her hand, John seated himself again. "Alright, Hon," he said, "let's study these properties, and see which one is the place where you want to raise our sons."

"Sons? Aren't you assuming? We don't know what this little one is yet." Charlotte patted her slightly rounded front as John grinned at her.

Another stomping of hooves and a low moo recalled the two to the order of the day. John sighed as he handed the papers back to his wife, instructing her to take them into the house and put them atop the breadbox with the other important papers. He would come in after finishing the milking and separating the cream. There was much to do today, and it wasn't getting done any faster with all this hugging and celebrating. Although usually quite practical, John had about forgotten himself with all this crying and suspense.

As Charlotte headed for the house, she tucked the papers back into the envelope, a bit crinkled now, with all that hugging. She wouldn't regret the hugs. Her life held too few of them. It was hard for her to believe that this was truly going to be a reality. Unless a terrible piece of land was apportioned to them, it looked as though they really would be trading this rented prairie land of Kansas for a "plat" of their own in rugged Wyoming territory.

The trail leading to this letter had been so lengthy and so full of complications that it had begun to feel like a dream and a test that they had to endure, in order to learn the ways of God and how He intended a man and wife to get along. Now, they really would be getting a fresh start to making a living on their very own land. Homesteaders! Why, this sounded so much like the stories about the settlers and the pilgrims. And to think— this really was her life!

Charlotte was so lost in thought, she almost stepped on the cat that dashed across her path and stood mewing at its dish, in hopes that her portion of milk might come early this morning. The slightly built young woman bent to pat the black-and-yellow speckled cat. "I know you're hungry, Specky. I've seen those five little kittens you have hidden in the shed. You'll just have to wait until the milking is finished. We kind of slowed it down this morning."

Kittens! Why, how many of the new little kittens would they take with them to Wyoming? And what would happen to the others? And would any of them still be kittens by the time John had built his family a house to live in?

"Mama, I'm hungry. It's thirteen o'clock. Come inside!" The three-year-old boy's voice wafted familiarly from the open front door of their unpainted frame house. As Charlotte smiled and waved to him, she reflected on what a good boy they had. They could leave the little tyke sleeping and get their chores mostly done because he knew to leave the stove alone and took great pride in following their directives. Many farm families had a tougher time than they did. Why, Donna had even told her how her little boy had eaten the goldfish right out of its bowl while she was trying to chore.

Kevin stepped with bare feet onto the worn and tilting wooden porch, ready for his mother's arms as she scooped up the warm and wiggling little body and carried him back into the house. What a wonder, how a man and woman's love for each other could merit a prize like this from God.

"Mama, what's that?" The tow-headed boy with the luminous blue eyes pointed to the white envelope peeping from her shirt pocket.

"Kev, my boy, this is a present from God. He has given us a chance to get a new house someday soon. We'll be living in a big house. Why, it might even have a bathroom in it!"

Kevin stared. His potty worked just fine while he was in the house. And the outhouse was nice enough in the summer. It did get cold in the winter, though. But a bathroom in the house would be like his grandma's in Kansas City. Sometimes Grandma would sit him up on the edge of that tall white potty and let him flush it afterwards. And, once he even got to take a bath in that big white tub with legs. He even got fresh bath water and didn't have to wait until after Mommy and Daddy were done. They wouldn't let him have the first bath now because he had pooped in their metal bathtub and "nastied up" the water. He saw that it took Mama a long time to heat enough water to fill that metal tub. A bathroom like Grandma's would be very fancy. Grandma's hot water came right out of those faucets.

*   *   *

John's hands pulled in rhythm, his shoulder shoving against the restless movement of the cow he squatted against. The ping-ping of the milk's stream hit the bubbling froth in the bucket again and again. The movement of a cat beginning to creep around the barn's doorway drew John's gaze, and without missing his rhythm, he shot a stream of milk into the cat's face. Darting back to the doorway, the cat sat down, eagerly rubbing her paws across her face and licking them, carefully washing her face so that she might not miss any of the warm milk that dripped from her whiskers.

The Browns

Sophia shook her head, bouncing her blond curls. As she sat at the kitchen table, her gaze took in the blue-and-white checkered ruffled curtains at the kitchen window and the matching crocheted dishcloth and potholders hanging from the porcelain hooks above the kitchen sink. This could not be true. She had married a soldier,

seriously displeased. Sometimes it confused him how a man was supposed to get anything practical done and yet still please such a delightful whimsical darling.

"But, Precious," he began tentatively, "this is the before picture. You have to imagine it after we've made our mark. It's like a dress you would sew while it is still hanging on its bolt in the fabric store. This is the formless, unpatterned, unsewn version. It's up to you and me, Sweetie, to decide on the pattern we want our farm to take."

Flora sniffed. She glared at the prairie dog poking his head up from the very, very flat drab ground. It was hard to imagine bluebells and daffodils growing in this desolate place.

"You are comparing it to a bolt of fabric. It looks more like an old flour sack to me!" Her voice was carefully quiet.

"We'll put the house over there. And the barn will go there." Henry cast a sideways glance at Flora to see if his young wife was up to the next bit of information. "We'll need to put up fences before we get any livestock. They could wander off and be eaten by coyotes or mountain lions."

Flora's eyes went wide. "Coyotes and mountain lions? Don't they eat people?" She folded her arms across her chest, in her fake fur coat.

Henry sighed. His little wife was really a big-city girl. He wondered if she could make the switch to this land, which even he could see would be hard, would test his very manhood. "No, Honey, probably they do well to make off with a chicken here and there. Actually, you have more to fear from the rattlers than those other animals."

Flora turned on her heel. One hand was holding down her hat and the other was clapped over her mouth as she headed for their 1948 Plymouth. Her quick steps wove around the cactus that tried to grab her ankles. Her hand came off her mouth and waved at the ground. "What if we step on a snake? Come on, Henry, Honey, it's windy. Let's view the rest from the car."

As Henry swung the car door shut after him, he could see it all in his mind's eye, and he tried again to help Flora dream with him. "The house and barn will need protection from the northern wind. We'll plant trees, lots of them. They'll make a windbreak and maybe we can even put some apple trees among them, though I'm not sure apple trees are really all that strong against some of these winter winds."

Flora turned up the heater in the car. It was only autumn, but she knew the winters in Wyoming would be treacherous. "Let's drive around awhile, and see if we can see any of our neighbors."

The car followed the dirt road for miles. There were no houses, not even any fences.

"Henry, what are those piles of dirt?" Flora had noticed the high mounds of soil that still looked fresh, with little roads appearing to go behind the mounds at times.

"They call them canals. The Bureau of Reclamation controls them. That's the way we water our crops here.

They bring irrigation water to us. Every tree we plant will need to be watered from those ditches." Henry looked out across the prairie and imagined the sweet-smelling clover fields that would grow after he began to flood the dry earth with life-giving water.

"Oh, look, Henry. That must be a neighbor. But look at that dinky little house." Flora's nose wrinkled.

A building with a slanted roof stood on the barren ground, just off the road. It was roughed in, studs standing bare in the sunlight, under a roof that resembled the lean-to porch on Henry's and Flora's place back home. As Henry rolled the car to a stop, he could tell by the studs that this was to be a one-room house. An unpainted, but apparently finished outhouse stood behind the little building. A small pup tent stood close to the outhouse. The old green truck in the roughly mashed-down dirt driveway had its door open, and a young man could be seen drinking from his canteen inside.

As Henry stepped from his car, the man swung his leg down out of the truck.

"Hey, what d'you know?" the young man greeted Henry. Henry strode towards him while Flora tried to hear without hanging her head clear out of the window of their car. They mustn't be able to say that the man from Pennsylvania had a "gawker" for a wife.

"I'm John Elwood. Are you from around here?" John wiped his hand on his jeans and stuck it out, offering a firm handshake. His direct gaze stared into the green eyes of the red-haired man who appeared to be prematurely balding.

Grasping his hand, Henry could tell from the hard calluses that this man had moved far beyond just the dreaming and planning stage that he and Flora were still in. "Looks like we'll be neighbors; we're homesteading about four miles back east of here. My wife and I are from Pennsylvania. Zanders is the name. Henry Zanders."

John grinned. "My wife Charlotte will be mighty pleased to hear there are real people and an actual woman in the hereabouts."

Henry looked around. "Where is your wife? Charlotte, you say?"

John reached down and pulled a dried weed stem from the dirt and began to chew it. "My wife and son are still in Kansas. I'm pretty much staying in that tent over there while I get our house done. We're hoping to be all moved in before the hard snows fall."

John gazed at the sky and kicked at the ground restlessly. "They say it can even snow in August here at times, and I must get my wife out here before there are such snow storms that I can't move the family. Charlotte's going to be giving us another young one soon."

Henry stared. Now, this was a brave man! And from the looks of things, a talented one, too. That house was not going up like any amateur's. "What will you do for drinking water, John?"

John smiled. "I have me a well. We'll have water in the kitchen. I'm pretty good at spotting wells. Runs in the family. They call it 'witching.' Just requires a good willow twig." John's laugh rang out. "Finding that willow tree was the hardest part. Did you ever see a land with so few trees?"

Henry knew that he and Flora would have plenty to talk about as they headed back to the little town of Pavillion. He wasn't sure how Flora would feel about spending time with someone who considered himself a witch. Although he must admit, he'd known other people to swear by that willow-twig way of finding water.

"Well, John, I'd better get out of here and let you get back to work before the weather catches up with you. I'll be sending for Flora to be moving out here next summer from Pennsylvania by way of train. We'll look forward to getting to know you then. What would be your advice about what I should be working on first between now and then?"

John's forehead drew together thoughtfully. "Well, you might check to see if there are any more barracks you can tear down to use for lumber for your house. They're letting us scavenge the barracks from those Japanese concentration camps, as long as they last, to improve our homesteads. Not much in 'em worth having other than the lumber."

Henry thanked young Mr. Elwood and waved as he drove away. "Well, what did he say?" asked Flora in her usual quizzical way.

"He said he's a witch building a house from a concentration camp. And I think he's going to be a really good man to try to be just like."

CHAPTER 2

Through the Eyes of a Child

CHARLOTTE HELD HER abdomen, feeling the twinges inside. This rough old road might bring on an early delivery. John shifted the gear down, his elbow barely missing their son's small sleeping body, which was curled up between them. Kevin's eyes fluttered briefly and he sighed as he nestled anew against Charlotte's lap. John's and Charlotte's eyes met and they smiled knowingly, seeing the boy's head having such little room, with the new baby pressing ever more outward.

"Charlotte, it's going to get very rough up ahead," John nearly shouted over the noise of the truck. "I think I'll stop and let you out. You can walk down through the creek and meet me ahead. Take it slow, Hon. Maybe we can keep from jarring that kid loose inside you." As the truck pulled to a complete stop, Kevin wiggled to an upright position, rubbing his eyes.

"Stay in here, Kev," John directed. "Mommy needs a walk, but you need to help Daddy." Charlotte's legs felt strange as she swung to the ground and slammed the heavy truck door. She watched the loaded, swaying truck move down the hill over the ruts in the narrow road. Pulling her tweed coat tighter, she started downward, glimpsing the stream of water across the road at the bottom. Swinging her arms and rolling her tense neck, she breathed in the scent of sagebrush on the crisp autumn air.

"Oh! My sewing machine!" she called frantically as the truck lurched and several things toppled off the back from underneath the torn canvas cover. John wasn't stopping; he was shifting again, attempting to get back up the other side of the creek bank. Charlotte took a swift step forward before she calmed her urge to run and check her belongings. Her first job now was to steer her lumbering body in such a way as to protect this baby. This was truly a prairie—dirt and sagebrush and cactus in every direction. Oh, there was one tree over there in the distance. There must be a ditch nearby. Trees didn't grow here without watering.

John had stopped the truck at the top of the hill and was lifting Kevin down to the ground. Charlotte could tell that he didn't realize the load had shifted. She had just reached the fallen items herself, kneeling to examine the sewing machine. Its cabinet had suffered a broken leg, but all else looked intact. Good. She had lots to sew.

John said she would be making canvas dams for the irrigation system, as well as all the clothes and curtains.

"Charlotte, is it ruined?" John strode towards the pile. "Sorry, Hon," he said. "I was just afraid the old truck might not get back up that incline."

She shook her head. "Nothing you can't fix, just a broken leg on the sewing machine cabinet. And look, here's the potty chair, and some old rugs."

Kevin was pointing at the familiar enamel potty and holding his front. John saw Charlotte's glance and took the child's hand. "Come on, Kevin," he smiled, giving a wink at his wife. "Let me show you how Wyoming men water the cactus."

Soon the canvas top was freshly strapped down and the truck was headed back towards the little home on which John had worked so hard for his family. Charlotte was bracing herself. She knew it would look primitive, and she wouldn't hurt her husband for the life of her. He would be watching her face for the slightest twinge of disappointment. As her eyes looked straight ahead down the dirt road, Charlotte inwardly prayed, "Lord, help me show him that I am proud of his willingness to carve out this farm, our farm, from this desert land."

"Daddy, what's that, a puppy?" As Kevin stood on the seat between them, his small finger pointed at a blond-colored animal standing on its hind legs, head cocked as though smelling the air. Charlotte was awaiting his answer, too.

John laughed, so proud of this land that was now his own community. "It's a prairie dog, Kevin. They live in the ground in little tunnels they dig. They're scared of people. You'll never be able to touch one." His mother watched their son's expression. She knew he was making his own plans, thinking his own thoughts: "I will too touch one!"

With one arm resting on the windowsill of the truck and the other holding tightly to the wheel, John's shoulder nudged his toddler, and he said in a somber voice, "Kevin, you must stay away from holes in the dirt. Some are holes where the prairie dogs live, but others have snakes living in them."

"Yes, Dear. Please do tell him more about the snakes," Charlotte shivered. This would be a hard land in which to keep little ones safe.

"They're called rattlesnakes, Kevin. The snakes have a rattle on their tail. It doesn't look like a baby rattle, though. It's just about this long." John held his thumb and forefinger about an inch and a half apart. "When the snake senses danger, it shakes that rattle on the end of its tail and then it strikes. That means the snake reaches way far out, really fast, and bites, hard." He glanced at Kevin intently. "Kevin, a rattler bite can kill a big man. We always stay far away from snakes."

Kevin's eyes were open wide. Charlotte was glad his daddy was giving him this instruction. The child always thought Daddy's words were more important than Mommy's. What a pity, though; one more bit of innocence lost in order to keep the wee ones safe.

"We're almost there." John pulled the knob to turn on the headlights for the truck. "It's starting to get dark.

I had hoped to let you see the place for the first time in the daylight." Charlotte again heard in his voice how important it was that she approve of his efforts.

"Daddy, I want our house to be a blue house!" Kevin declared. John laughed.

"Too late, Kev, my boy. All the houses out here are just covered in tarpaper. And tarpaper is green."

John shifted down as they rounded the corner. "There, Charlotte, there's the house. It's just a one-roomer, but it's nice and sturdy and the cold wind can't howl through. By the time the three years is up, I'll have built you a nice big one with its own bathroom and maybe we'll even buy one of those modern refrigerators."

Charlotte sat forward. The truck lights didn't show any house. Wait! There was a little dirt driveway and the truck lights finally shone on the freshly built cabin.

"Daddy! Mommy! It's blue. My new house is blue!" Kevin was jumping up and down on the seat, with his mother's arm thrown out in front of his little knees.

"My! I've never noticed that before." John's expression was one of awe as he parked the truck and sat with the headlights shining on the small building. "It does look blue. It must be the way the truck lights shine on it."

"Honey! It's wonderful. It's a sign. God is showing us it is everything we want and need! Hurry, come and show me our wonderful little house!" *Bless you, Lord*, Charlotte thought. *Trust You to let me look at my husband's workmanship through the eyes of a child.*

John was grinning as he set the boy on the ground and slammed the truck's door. He waited proudly as

go get that bag in the truck. It's on the floorboards. I have some peanut butter and jelly sandwiches left. I even have some powdered milk in there. We'll have supper."

John nodded. Supper. His family, here beside him. As he headed back out into the night, which was getting chillier by the second, he heard the now-familiar sound of yelping coyotes. Finally. This could be home now. If only they had one big bed for tonight. Oh, well, he'd been waiting patiently for a number of months now. One more night wouldn't hurt.

CHAPTER 3

A Bright Spot

SOPHIA RUBBED THE sleep from her eyes and sat up. Georgie had awakened her. "Mommy, Mommy," he was calling. She looked at the empty pillow beside her. It was still dark but Jack had already left the cabin. Of course, Jack called it "our house," but to Sophia it was nothing more than an old shack. She slid her sock-clad feet out of the bed onto the wooden floor. She could feel the chill straight through the cotton socks. "Mommy. Mommy." She followed the sound. She could tell her son was growing excited that his mommy was nearing. He was shaking the rails of the crib now.

She reached her arms down around his little body, and could feel the dampness of his pajama bottoms. How did he continuously wet clear around the elastic legs of his rubber pants? Now she would no doubt need to change the sheets of his baby bed as well. More wash for the Monday laundry! At least she didn't have to rub the sheets on the washboard to get them clean. Now, Jack's work pants! That was another story.

The boy whimpered when his mother set him back onto his feet on the damp mattress. Sophia took a few steps to her right and reached around and touched the lantern. She felt beside it for the box of matches she had set out the night before. It was an important habit by now to be sure the lamp was full of fuel, the wick up, and matches laid out. She did it every night right after her final drink from the big dipper in the water pail. Jack promised the electric company would be out soon to hook up their power.

Picking up the lantern, she carried it from the draining board to the dresser top. Georgie's little face was laughing up at her as she bent and caught him up in her arms. He was placing his wet little lips against her cheek as she slid him down onto her hip and reached for fresh diapers, rubber pants, a new pair of pajamas and a receiving blanket. She smiled into his little face as she laid him down onto her bed to change him. "Your momma loves you. Yes, she does. You are a good, good boy."

Grabbing the wet things from her bed, she carried them and the squirming boy over to the two buckets. The one without a lid was for the regular clothes, and the diaper pail had the lid. Tossing the pajamas into the first bucket, she leaned to lift the lid from the second one. "Phew, Georgie, that's a stinky bucket." She was quick to drop the diaper and lower the lid. Her hands were stinging and cracked from scrubbing strong-smelling diapers in bleach and detergent.

Sophia was snuggled again in her bed with their child at her breast when she heard the door open and Jack came stomping in, onto the rag rug. "Morning!" he called. "You should see that sunrise out there!" He strode to the table and placed the bucket of milk on it. "Makes me want to hurry up and get a rooster!"

"Is there ice on the water trough?" Sophia wondered how cold it had been last night. She knew Jack would already have lit a match to the thermometer hanging on the porch to see.

"Nope. The cow drank the water easily enough. Still nice enough weather to dig more fence post holes. We'll bundle Georgie up after breakfast and put him in his walker while you help me dig some."

"Yippee," Sophia thought to herself wryly. Just what every woman dreams of: Getting up in a shack with no electricity, pulling a snowsuit onto a toddler, and helping step onto a post- hole-digger.

Jack leaned over her and kissed her forehead. "I'm a lucky man, Darlin'! You make a very pretty picture there with our son!"

Sophia smiled. Her soldier still sounded the same, even wearing these farmer clothes. He was a happy fellow these days, and she couldn't help but feel some of his excitement. His glittery blue eyes always melted her inside.

Jack took off his jacket and hung it on the nail behind the door. He stoked up the fire and put a pan of water on top to boil. He called out, "Oatmeal okay?" He set a clean quart jar in the dishpan. Striding to the table he carried the bucket of warm milk over to the dishpan and began to pour it carefully into the quart jar. He reached for a second jar and finished pouring the bubbly milk into it. He slid the two jars into the icebox, checking to see if the chunk of ice was still sufficient.

"When we go into Pavillion tomorrow, we'll need to get another block of ice." Pavillion had only a hundred or so people, but it did have a gas station and a grocery store. It had a bar, of course, but Jack knew that his dreams and drinking didn't go hand in hand. And it had an ice locker where one could keep frozen quarters of beef.

Sophia spread a blanket on the floor and put some of Georgie's painted wooden blocks on it. Setting the boy down with his favorite squeaker toys, she pulled a robe around her. "I want us to look again at the church in town and see what time it starts. I think we should be in church on Sunday."

Jack grinned. "Gonna wear those high-heeled shoes there, aren't you, Love?"

*　　*　　*

Their green 1947 Ford churned up quite a dust storm on the dirt road as they drove to Pavillion on Saturday. Georgie slept across Sophia's lap. Jack downshifted, slowing the car, and pointed at the "homestead improvements" that were happening along the road. "Look, Sophia, Henry Zander has poured his concrete foundation. Looks like he plans to build a two-bedroom house before he moves his wife out here! He said he will get as far as he can before the snow drives him back to Pennsylvania for the winter."

Sophia pulled her sweater tighter. "When does it start snowing out here? Did they-all ever tell you?"

Jack smiled. He knew the "all" didn't have to mean plural. His Oklahoma bride's dialect was an amusement to him. On this homestead, there was sure to be a mixture of accents and speech patterns. People had applied to homestead from all different parts of the country. An honorable discharge from the military was the one feature most of the men had in common, plus their ability to plan and be able to pay for the "improvements" that were required as their part of the homestead agreement.

"We're past the time when it first snows some years, Sophia." Jack had shifted back up through the gears again, and they were going thirty miles an hour down the dirt road! "I'm told it can snow in August here. We are really getting some extensions on the nice weather this year."

Georgie giggled in his sleep. His parents cast a glance at him, then their eyes met in appreciation. "I suppose we should get a sled to pull him on, so he can have nice memories of growing up in Wyoming," said Sophia.

"Maybe for Christmas, Dear," Jack said absently. Sophia secretly hoped they would have electric lights by then. She wanted to pull out her favorite Christmas tree ornaments, the ones that bubbled when plugged in.

They rode in silence for awhile, Jack lost in plans of all he wanted to get done before the snow fell, feeling a bit resentful of having to drive into town for supplies on such a nice day. Sophia was a good sport, but she drew the line at driving to town by herself.

"Look! The Elwoods are out on their North 40! Let's stop and say hi," said Sophia excitedly. Jack nodded and began to slow the car.

Georgie was awake by the time his father had turned off the motor. Sophia adjusted the earmuffs over his ears and zipped the hood from his coat up over them. The little mittens, hanging from his sleeves on a string, were harder to put on, over his wiggling fingers. Jack came around to the passenger side and opened her door. She believed he might be the only "farmer" out here who displayed such gallantry.

It was chilly outside as they crossed the lateral ditch and moved across the ground to where the Elwood family was kneeling, all bending over some project.

"Hey! What d'you know?" John was on his feet now, beating the dirt from his knees. Charlotte's wool bandanna was knotted under her chin, and she stayed hunched over, with their son, holding steady a twig of a tree. Charlotte had adapted well to the country; she wore men's gloves and boots. Little Kevin held a coffee can.

"Go ahead, Kevin, water it now," Charlotte commanded the boy. Kevin peeked at the company and importantly strode to the water bucket sitting on the prairie. He dipped in the red coffee can and came back to pour it onto the little bare-root tree.

"What are you doing there, Kevin?" Jack asked the boy.

"We're planting a windbreak. This one is a sand-cherry tree. Mommy says she will make me sand-cherry ice cream from it some day."

John chuckled. "Nothing grows without water around here. It'll probably be a few years before these trees outgrow Kevin. But, we'll sure be glad when it keeps the north wind from cutting through the house. The new house should sit about over there."

Charlotte arose. Her pregnancy protruded from the front of her coat. "Sophia. Georgie. So good to see you. You headed to Pavillion?"

"We have to get some things. We're almost out of ice at home."

Charlotte smiled and said, "We don't have to use ice. The well pit is cold enough that we just lower things down on a rope."

Kevin's eyes were big: "I have to be careful. I would hurt really bad if I fell down the well pit."

John patted his shoulder. "You're a good boy, son. So, how are you coming out your way, Jack, with the fence?"

"It's pretty slow. I have the cow corral done and Sophia and I are trying to finish what will be a pasture. It's a shame to cut the work short and head for town on a nice day like this one."

John looked somberly at Jack. "I had a dream last night. I talked about it already with my wife, but I'd like to talk with you about it, too. What do you think, could you folks come over to the house tomorrow, for Sunday dinner?"

"Yes, please do come for dinner. I will make a meatloaf and some baked potatoes and we can eat about one o'clock," Charlotte sounded eager for company.

Jack put his arm around his wife's shoulders and looked down into her hopeful face. "What do you think?" Her blond curls were moving up and down and her eyes were glowing as Jack answered for the two of them, "We'll be happy to come."

Sophia added, "I'll bring some fresh sliced peaches for dessert. We got a half bushel in town last week. I've been canning them. And, I'll bring thick cream to pour over them."

"Mmmm," John and Charlotte said in unison.

The men reached out to grip each other's hand in a calloused handshake and the women smiled, as Sophia hitched Georgie up a notch on her hip. "See you tomorrow," said Jack, steadying his wife as she stepped around a cactus on the way back across the sagebrush-strewn ground to their car.

John turned back to his bundle of saplings. There were more alongside the south side of the house at home. He paced another four feet and shoved the spade into the ground with his foot. Several shovelfuls of dirt later, he paused while Charlotte cut open the burlap from the roots, and pushed another tree into the brown soil. She picked up two of the short wooden stakes and formed a northwest corner with them as she pushed them in around the new tree. John was pressing the freshly dug soil back around the twig when Kevin arrived with his can of water to pour onto the mound.

"It'll be nice to have company," Charlotte's said, her voice husky. She was glad she had taken the hamburger from the locker in town earlier this week and had lowered it into the well pit to thaw. She would have had to use it tomorrow anyway or it would go bad. She thought she had just about enough of the biscuits left that she'd made yesterday. Maybe she'd spread out the tablecloth that Mama had made for her just before she left home.

It would be their first real company since they'd moved here. Just so this baby didn't decide to come for the occasion, too.

CHAPTER 4

A Team

"**I** HAVE BEEN quite curious about your dream, John," Jack said, handing his plate over to Charlotte as she gathered their dinner plates from the table. Sophia stood to help her neighbor. But, she stacked the dishes quietly, making sure she could hear what the men were discussing. It had the sound of importance.

"Well, I was dreaming that I bought a tractor and a plow, and a cultivator, and a planter; and I put in some alfalfa. I irrigated it and even got snake-bit a time or two that summer. But when the hay was ready to be cut and baled, I didn't have the implements. I couldn't figure out how to get the hay out of the fields. It was all going to be covered by the winter snows." John stopped for emphasis, took a drink from his water glass.

"And in the dream, you and Sophia were very upset. You had the best kind of corn seed for planting silage, but you only had a combine and a hay-baler! So, you were down in the dumps and I was plumb crazy with concerns." John leaned forward and looked at his new friend across the table. One man's piercing brown eyes gazed into the other man's glittering blue ones.

John could hear the little boys playing on the wooden floor nearby, rolling the toy metal truck back and forth. The women had stopped scraping and clattering the dishes. John knew all the adults were staring straight at him.

"Jack, I think we should each make our money stretch further. I think it is a waste if I buy a plow and a planter, and you also buy a plow and a planter. What if I bought half the farm implements I need to fully farm this place, and you buy the other half? We'd have to be plumb neighborly and make sure we were good about sharing the equipment and taking care of it. The way I have it figured, if I own an implement, it is my responsibility to be getting it all ready for spring during the winter. But if I am borrowing your piece of equipment, and I break it, then it is for me to fix it … as long as you truly have done your best to keep the implement in top shape." He pushed his chair back and tipped it onto its back legs. "What do you think?"

Jack stared. The old cuckoo clock on the wall struck two, and the bird darted out to yell twice. Then quiet, except for the "udden, udden" sound of the boys playing with their pretend trucks. Jack turned his chair to look at

Sophia. She had tears on her cheeks, and a sweet smile on her lips.

Jack turned back to John. "I think, my friend, that we just might be able to make this work. I made a promise to God when He let me get this homestead plat: I told Him I would work the land in His spirit. If we keep that in mind about pleasing God, we surely could be neighborly about the way we took turns using our equipment."

Sophia's face grew pink and she reached out a hand and placed it on Jack's shoulder. Her other hand had already been taken and was being squeezed gently by smiling Charlotte, who had tears twinkling in her own blue eyes.

It was again quiet, except for the two little boys clinking their metal trucks on the wooden floor and making pretend motor sounds, "Udden, udden!"

CHAPTER 5

A Man's Work

HENRY LIFTED ANOTHER log into place. He had developed quite a good strategy. He slid one end onto his scaffold, and then went around to the other end and hoisted it up so the log could be rolled onto the wall. This seemed to him to be the fastest way to build a sturdy house that would keep out the winter winds. Sure, he still had to caulk it, but it was encouraging to watch his house take shape. There would be an inside bathroom. Not any primitive outhouse for his high-strung Flora.

Thinking about bathrooms made him long for one. He went over and stood with his back to the truck and relieved himself. A pheasant cock scuttled around the front of the truck. Darn! If he'd had his twenty-two rifle, he'd have had a tasty dinner!

Henry strode across the concrete floor and brought out his level, laying it across the top of the latest log. Except for the lack of uniformity in the logs, this was going up pretty level. He pried his scaffold up another notch, first at one end, then the other. He wasn't sure that Flora would be so happy about the lack of windows along this north wall, but he wasn't taking any chances. He had heard enough stories about it being so cold here in Wyoming that the windows became completely covered with ice on the north side of the house. Storm windows could only help so much. They'd have windows on the other sides of the house. The western windows would be risky enough!

Whistling as he worked, he moved from end to end of the logs, grunting as he heaved each end up to the platform from which he then rolled it into place. Good thing he had those brace boards up on the back side.

What was that sound? He paused. Hearing a vehicle coming down the road, he stopped his work and went to get a canteen from the truck, drinking deeply from it before he sat on the front seat, opened his lunch box, and took out the apple and his jelly sandwich. Man, he missed Flora's cooking. Say, that looked like the mail car coming and he might get a letter from Flora!

The familiar black 1948 Ford stopped at his mailbox. The mailman put some white squares in the metal box and slammed it shut. Rolling down his window, old Harvey called out to Henry, "Looking good, Henry. That wall's come up a lot from yesterday!"

Henry waved and grinned before wiping his mouth across the wristband of his knit sleeve. He stood up from the vehicle and left the door open. He might have to turn the motor on and heat it up if he was going to keep still long enough to read the mail. He pulled open the mailbox and looked inside. He knew better than to reach into it without looking. There could be any manner of scorpion or snake anyplace out here. Hmmm … a letter from his mother in Boston, and a letter from the bank, and there! There was a letter from Flora with lipsticked kiss marks on the back. No wonder the mailman had smiled so much at him today. Henry glanced down the road, with an embarrassed grimace.

He went back to the truck and started the motor, pulled on the emergency brake, and turned down the heater fan, which was just blowing out cold air.

"Dear Henry, I miss you so much. I cannot believe we can be okay and continue to live apart like this. I ache inside so deeply without you. I have been trying to sort through things and see what I really can do without, so we can give some things away before we come out there. No point in packing things we will just leave in boxes. I have also been sewing. I have made a pretty new scarlet dress with puffed sleeves, and a black and scarlet coat to wear over it. You recall I have those nice black high-heeled pumps I can wear with it. I also sewed you up a Western shirt out of some of the material I used to make the coat. We can go in style to that country church, matching!"

Henry shook his head. She was such a sweet female, but she hadn't quite gotten into the mindset of this rugged country. Oh, well. He could probably leave a day of cutting out a farm from this dirt and sagebrush and head to church in a matching outfit with his lovely lady.

"I have some bad news, I'm sorry to say. Our neighbor's little girl, Daphne, has polio. She is in a huge iron lung in Pittsburgh. They say if she lives, she could be paralyzed."

Henry cursed. That little girl, only about five, was as cute as they come. This polio thing was becoming a real nightmare. He'd heard a man at the gas filling station here talking about another little kid, about 20 miles out, who also had been diagnosed with polio. It made him afraid to shoot and eat the rabbits. Some folks said it was the fleas on the rabbits that carried polio.

He sure hoped they found the cause or a cure before he brought Flora out here.

"I have made some really pretty tablecloths and cloth napkins so that we will have a lovely table when I arrive there. I put together some artificial flower arrangements because I want flowers in the middle of the table. I have been collecting some seed packets so that I can plant some flowers for us; then maybe I can cut some of our own flowers for the center pieces."

What odd things women think about when preparing to move to this primitive place!

"Well, Darling, you say you miss me and our warm bed. I cannot imagine how you stay warm way out there, huddled in your little shack. But, please do come back as soon as you can, because I miss you so much that I am about to wear out your picture. Love, Flora."

Henry smiled and carefully folded the pages, and put the letter, with the others, in the truck's glove compartment.

As he turned off the motor, he realized the engine had just barely started to warm up the cab. He strode over to the little "shack" that Flora spoke of. It wasn't much more than that. He had built himself a hut that was little bigger than a dog house. It pretty much worked like one. He just had room for a wooden crate and a bedroll inside. It kept out the infrequent rain, the cold winds and the coyotes. He warmed up in the truck when it was just too cold. All his cooking was done on the outdoor campfire. He reached his arm into the wooden box inside the hut and got a beer. Sometimes a guy just needed cheering up.

CHAPTER 6

Priorities

"IT'S CALLED THE FHA … Farmers Home Administration … It's the way we will have to make our money stretch here, Charlotte." John was trying to be patient. "I know you don't like to owe anyone. I don't either." He put his arm around her shoulder.

"John, it worries me. I saw my parents lose everything because when there was a poor crop, they had to pay all the money to the bank." A tear slid down Charlotte's cheek. "Then there was no money for the next year's seed, and no money to deliver my little sister. The neighbor lady tried to do the midwifing, but little Sally was born dead. It brings back lots of bad memories …"

"Hon, I know that's the way it was for your family. But the FHA is all about helping us make a go of our farm here. Jack and I sat down and talked with them, and he and I have tried to weigh all the pros and cons. You and I only have two hundred dollars left, and Jack has a hundred-fifty. Look, to repair the radio cost more than six dollars last week. We couldn't go any longer without hearing the weather forecasts. Besides, I saw you looking at the clock when it would have been time for "Fibber McGee's Closet!"

Charlotte felt a bit more cheered. She straightened her shoulders. John did notice the little things about her.

"And, getting new tires for the truck was fifty-nine dollars and some odd change … The light bill was three dollars and fifty-seven cents …" John began striding about the kitchen with his right arm held behind his back with the other. A sure sign of intensity. "Jack got the last implement, a combine, for eight hundred fifty dollars! You know that means we buy the next piece of equipment. Hon, it's just plumb necessary that we get a loan to get this farm off the ground right."

"Well," Charlotte conceded, "can we at least pray about it first?"

John stopped his pacing. He took his stained felt hat from the chair where he'd tossed it when he came in out of the cold. "Yes. I'll go pray while I break the ice from the cow's trough, and you do your praying in here by the fire." He was pulling his gloves from his pocket as he went out and let the door slam behind him.

Charlotte knew he didn't mean to sound sarcastic. She did get to have a warmer time of it in their little one-room home. She was spending much of her time keeping

Kevin occupied in the small space, and was into that time only a woman knows, of feeling a little like a mare about to foal, sort of drawn into herself and protecting her young colt.

"Mama," Kevin's sleepy voice called out from beneath the heavy quilt on her bed, "can I get up now?" Another nap finished. And, she had hoped to lie down to rest beside the small boy. Not today.

Suddenly her back felt as though an axe had come down on it. Charlotte bent over, and grabbed for the back of the nearby kitchen chair. After what seemed like forever, the pain began to ebb but left her with a nauseous stomach. Her eyes sought the clock.

"Get up, Kevie. Come to mom. Bring your shoes, Sweetie," she managed to say in a normal voice. She eyed the clock. Six minutes passed before the pain wrenched her again. She lowered her swollen body down into the chair.

"Mommy. Mommy. What's wrong?" Kevin was peering up into her grimacing face. He wrapped his chubby arms around his mother to make her all better with his hug.

With deep breaths, Charlotte passed the seconds. "Now, Honey, get your overshoes and pull your coat down from the nail. Mommy wants to get you ready for an outside job." Glancing over his shoulder at his mother, who wasn't acting quite right, Kevin hurried to bring his outdoor things. Charlotte was free again of the pains and quickly pulled on the boy's overshoes and coat, finishing by maneuvering his hands into the mittens.

Pulling the striped stocking cap over his little ears, she said urgently, "Now, run and get Daddy. He is down at the cow's trough. Tell him Mama says, "It's time." Can you tell me what you must tell Daddy?"

"Mama says it's time!" Kevin clearly repeated.

"Yes, perfect." The clock said it had now been seven minutes before the next pain was starting. "Come right back if you don't find Daddy there!"

The door slammed behind the boy, as Charlotte stood to head for the bed. Sitting on it, she waited for the latest hatchet to come away from her back. Finally, with a vile taste in her mouth, she leaned down to pull the satchel from beneath the bed. She unzipped it and made sure she had remembered to pack everything. There was her pretty new lavender bed jacket, and the little pink dress if it were to be a girl and a blue romper if it were to be a boy. And the lovely crocheted yellow blanket and sweater with hat and mittens her mother had made for the new baby–after she'd finished being upset that her daughter would be coming out to this far-away forsaken land to have babies!

The door burst open and Kevin flew in before John stomped off the snow and entered. "We started the truck, Mama. Daddy says I get to stay at Georgie's for the night!"

John stood over Charlotte, his eyes warm with concern. "What shall I pack for Kevin?"

Charlotte sat with a rigid expression on her face, making no real sound. Little Kevin pulled his cardboard suitcase from under the bunk bed. He snapped it open. "Look! It's all packed," he exclaimed.

John pulled back the sheet that hung down across a corner of the room near their double bed. He brought Charlotte's wool plaid coat from the wooden rod he had fastened across that corner. "Anything else I need to do?" he asked her uncertainly.

"A couple towels. Get some clean towels. Just in case. They're coming pretty close together."

John's brow furrowed. Forty-five miles to the hospital seemed a long ways on this cold winter day. "Carry your suitcase, Kevin," he directed, and used the poker to scatter the embers in the wood stove. He threw in another couple of sticks, put his arm through Charlotte's, and asked, "Ready?"

Charlotte nodded and leaned against him as she rose from the bed, buttoning her coat. She pulled an envelope from her pocket and handed it to John. "It's the hundred dollars we saved for this. But it probably won't take it all!"

"A hundred dollars. Wow!" Even Kevin knew that was a very big sum. He ran alongside his mom and dad, as his father's big fist stuffed the money into his overhaul's pocket.

They passed the ruffled bassinet as the three of them headed to the door. As Kevin marched out, John flipped the switch to the light, darkening the room. Joining his growing family in the crisp October air, he pushed the door to make sure it had latched. No one knew where the key was anymore. It didn't matter. People had better things to do in this rough country than to steal from each other.

CHAPTER 7

A Letter from the Sticks

"DEAR FLORA: I sure do miss you. I guess our Third Division Homestead Project population is growing. I have seen a couple other vehicles driving around, and some men standing out in the snow looking around. Maybe they are trying to figure out if their wives are as brave as mine! And, we have a newcomer here. Do you recall John? He's the one who "witched" his well! Good water, too, I hear. He and Charlotte have the little boy, Kevin. Well, Charlotte had her baby, a girl. I know you'll want to know the baby's name, but I cannot recall it, something like Delores, or Dorothy or such. But, John is going around all proud of himself.

Our log home has a roof on it now. I put tarpaper on the sheeting. The winter's cold enough that the shingles wouldn't stick, so I'll have to plan to pull up the paper on the roof and put down more when it warms up in April or so. Hopefully, it'll at least keep the snow from piling up inside our house. It is way too cold to fill in the chinks between the logs with tar now, so I'll have to let that go until spring. In fact, I really can't do much out here for the rest of the winter now; it is just way too cold for me in my "shack" as you call it.

So, I am going on down to Oklahoma and try to get some work so that I will have money to do some more building when I get back here in the spring. When I was at the bar the other night, Horrace told me that the mine in Oklahoma is hiring right now. Don't worry, Dear; I will come back to Pennsylvania and be with you for Christmas. And Santy has a real gift for you. Do you have one for Santy? Love, Henry."

Flora laughed, then rested her head on her arms atop the letter lying on the table and sobbed. She sure hoped her farmer husband knew what he was doing. She didn't. She could use a good time of going dancing! And here she was, probably the prettiest girl on the block and the only one stuck home every night like an old maid! A car honked at something down on the street and Flora lifted her head to listen to the warm, familiar sound of city life.

CHAPTER 8

Friends Become Family

"IT WOULDN'T BE Christmas without company. Promise you'll come for Christmas dinner!" Sophia's gloved fingers pushed down the stocking cap more firmly over Georgie's forehead. "We'll be having turkey and cranberry sauce. Bring some of that scrumptious upside-down cake you bake."

Charlotte chuckled. Her breath came out in the December air in visible clouds. Her cake's reputation was bigger than her own in this homestead settlement, it seemed. A whimper rose from the blanket where she held Deirdre close to her chest. She cradled her baby closer in her arms. "Mama wonders how we will stand being 'all alone out there with the snakes and coyotes' for Christmas!" Charlotte laughed aloud now.

"Well, you don't have to be alone!" said Sophia. "And, I guess she doesn't know that the snakes hibernate in the winter! I know I was really scared of the rattlers when we moved here, too. I don't want Georgie to get bitten by one."

"Morning," Charlotte said, as she nodded to another woman walking past her on the sidewalk. There had been quite a few in church today, maybe thirty. Sophia looked nice in her red pumps, with her red and gray woolen coat and hat. Charlotte looked past her to the unknown woman's receding back. She must be from the irrigation project that was settled before their Third Division one had been. Perhaps she'd introduce herself next week.

Their truck began to approach, with Jack's green car coming behind it. The men had hurried out as soon as the church doors opened, to warm the vehicles. Kevin had insisted on being daddy's helper and going along, too. As John pulled alongside her, Charlotte smiled and said to her friend, "Yes, we will be there for Christmas dinner. I'll bring the cake, and my mother's custard pie, too. Now, what time do you want us?"

Jack had parked the car and was warning Georgie to stomp off the snow before getting into the back seat. "You better be a good boy. Santa is watching to see if you're naughty or nice." Georgie's little face glowed with excitement.

Charlotte watched as Jack placed his hand under Sophia's elbow and steered her into the front seat. "One o'clock. Come at one!" Sophia called to her.

John stayed firmly in the driver's seat, as Kevin stood up in the middle. Charlotte pulled the door open, maneuvering the baby as she slid in. She never questioned John's love, just his manners at times. "We'll have Christmas dinner with the Browns. They want us there at one o'clock." Her husband nodded. John let her make all the decisions about social invitations. As long as she allowed time for him to milk the two cows and do the choring, he wouldn't mind. Of course, she also had to plan time for the gift-opening, too, on Christmas day, because Kevin was now aware that Santa would be coming.

"Look, Charlotte. Last night's wind tore loose some of Zanders' roof paper. I'd better bring my hammer and roofing nails over and tap it back down before we eat today." No one had asked John to watch over his neighbor's place, but the Golden Rule was the code out here. He would have been mighty grateful if someone helped keep his place from deteriorating if he'd had to go to Oklahoma to earn money to keep things afloat!

"Daddy, do you thank Santa would bring me a puppy? I need a puppy to hug. I could teach him to warn us if a coyote was sneaking up on us …" Kevin laid his arm across his father's shoulder and stooped to peer seriously into his eyes.

John and Charlotte's gaze met over the child's head. John laughed and shifted into a higher gear. The whine left the transmission. The heater was finally blowing gusty warm air into the truck cab. "Coyotes are scared of us, Kev. We aren't scared of them! We probably need to wait until we have the 'big house' to get a dog, Kevin. Shall I help you catch a rabbit this spring?"

Charlotte watched the light fade from Kevin's face. It was hard to watch her son be disappointed. But she understood John's position. Dogs require food. They were rather concerned about their own food lasting all winter. It sure was good that she found those peaches and apricots for sale by the bushel last fall. She had many jars of canned fruit sitting on the shelves John had built. Maybe she could still find a stuffed dog in the Sears and Roebuck catalog for little Kevin.

CHAPTER 9

A Homestead Christmas

JOHN SLID FROM under the covers, grabbed the denim pants he'd laid next to the bed, and pulled them on over his long-johns. He quickly put his flannel shirt on over his tee shirt. Brrr! The garments would soon warm from his body heat. Having learned better than to take off his socks in these cold Wyoming winter nights, he padded across the chilled wooden floor to stoke up the fire. It was sure a good thing he'd kept every snaggled board from when he'd torn down that old barracks. He had built this little house with the good boards, but the poorer ones made great firewood. One just had to watch out for the nails sticking from them; it'd be easy for the kids to step on one!

John was anxious to see what was on the other side of the window. He'd need to scrape some ice from it, as the condensation was freezing over on it again. He grabbed the putty knife from the windowsill and began to slide it back and forth across the glass, trying not to make too much noise and awaken his wife. Charlotte had been up late last night, trying to lay out the Santa items without awakening the children. Sometimes it was challenging to carry on such things in a one-room home.

John stared through the peephole in the window. He'd known it was going to be quite a snowy sight, judging by the wintry sounds they'd heard during their Christmas preparations the previous evening. He truly was looking upon a "winter wonderland," just like the Christmas songs that had been playing on the radio! The wind had drifted the new snow, as it fell atop the earlier eight inches of snow already on the ground. Some of those drifts out there must be three feet tall.

Hmm. He wondered what this would do to their dinner plans. He hoped they would find the roads passable, as Charlotte would be disappointed not to be able to get to their friends' house for Christmas dinner. Womenfolk certainly did better when they could chatter to one another. And the smells of her baking still filled the air.

Shrugging into his winter coat, John pulled on his earmuffs and pulled the hood over his head. He stepped into the rubber hip-boots he'd gotten in preparation for next summer's irrigating, and tugged on his heavy leather gloves. It required some strength to push open the door against the snow that had drifted against it. John was sure glad he'd thought to put the door on the south side, so the north or west winds wouldn't blow through the cracks around the door!

He kicked his foot through the pile of snow alongside the door and found the scoop shovel that stood there, although it had blown down in the wind. He could see his breath in the air as he dug into the snow and cleared a path from the door to the outhouse, and then to the cow shed. The water trough was frozen over. Good thing he kept the sledgehammer next to it. Brushing off the snow, he cracked the ice and pulled it out, finding the water fresh underneath. The two cows stood close together in a corner of the shed. They appeared to be okay, free of snow where they stood. He smiled, remembering how the preacher had said on Sunday that we get one life to live, and that the new-fangled belief of reincarnation just isn't true. The preacher had laughed, asking the congregation how they'd like to look forward to coming back in a "second life" as a cow! John liked his manner of housing much better than the cows'! He kicked a hay bale from outside the fence and it still moved, not yet frozen to the ground. He heaved it over into the side with the cows, went around and pulled the binding twine from it, and kicked the hay apart with his boot. He stuffed the twine into his pocket. Who knew what use Charlotte would make of the twine, but she had quite a ball of it collected.

John was tempted to start the truck and try out the road, so he could see if there was something he could do to make it a surer thing that they could get to Jack and Sophia's for dinner today. But, his stomach's growling reminded him that there'd been no breakfast yet, and his wife would want him there when Kevin got up to see what Santa had left under their tree.

That tree had been quite an accomplishment! Just a little scrub cedar that had grown along the creek bank. But Charlotte had asked him to dig out her box of Christmas ornaments from the pile of boxes that lined one whole wall of their little home. Amazing, with the boxes stacked from floor to ceiling, that his wife had known just which box he must remove. And Charlotte had worked magic with the decorating of that little tree he'd chopped down. Kevin had been so excited, dancing around the ornate tree, and even little Deirdre's eyes had fastened, with apparent wonder, upon the twinkling lights.

The snow had stopped falling as John tromped his way back to the house, after making a stop at the outhouse. Welcoming smoke rose from the chimney, and he could smell the cornbread and bacon as he entered the house. Yum! One of his favorites, warm cornbread covered in butter and syrup! And bacon was a Christmas treat, kept cold enough in a wooden box outside the door, to keep coyotes and stray dogs from it. John stripped off his coat and hung it on a nail behind the door. He pulled off his boots and stood them on the tin cookie sheet they kept on the floor for that purpose. The house was warmer now.

Charlotte was dressed and wore her prettiest apron as she turned from the stove into his bear hug. "Merry Christmas, my dear!" She spoke into his chilled neck. "I think I'd better awaken Kevin if we are to do all these things we've planned today." Deirdre was making cooing sounds, and her hump of blankets was wiggling in the crib.

John retrieved the baby and a fresh diaper and brought her to Charlotte to change. He strode back to little Kevin, where he slept under heavy quilts in the army bunk bed that John had retrieved from the barracks. "Wake up, son. Santa's been here!" As Kevin leaped up, Charlotte moved quickly to the boy's side to throw a robe around his shoulders and slippers onto his stocking feet.

The Christmas tree's lights were plugged in and bubbling as Kevin raced to see what was underneath it. Charlotte was adhering to the family customs of generations, as she had placed their "Santa" gifts, unwrapped, under the tree.

"Oh, look! Santy brought me a doggie, after all!" Kevin hugged the black and white plush puppy to his chest. Charlotte sighed in relief. The Sears and Roebuck package had arrived only yesterday! "I'm going to name him Happy!" John was winking at Charlotte over Kevin's head.

"Look, Di Dee," said Kevin as he knelt to pick up a pull toy. "Santy's elves made you a teddy bear." He managed to hold up the brown stuffed bear to the baby with one hand as he tickled her tummy with the other.

"You're still little. That's why you have a little bear, and I have a big puppy."

"You'd better see if old Santa remembered to put something in your sock!" his daddy reminded Kevin. Charlotte had insisted everyone hang one of their clean socks on a new nail they'd hammered into the Celotex walls last night. Kevin raced to look inside his bulging, drooping sock. John helped him pull it from the nail, while he curiously pulled down his own. How does Charlotte do this? He hadn't seen her putting anything into the stockings.

Kevin emptied an apple, an orange, some peanuts in their shells, and chocolate drops and ribbon candy onto his little bed. And from the bottom of the sock, his little pudgy hand pulled a bag of marbles. "You'll have to be careful and pick up every one of them so the baby doesn't swallow any," Charlotte warned him.

John was sorting his sock-full of goodies onto the kitchen table. "Good! Brazil nuts, and peanuts, and ribbon candy. Chocolate, and look, Kevin, Daddy got a new pocket knife!" John grinned at Charlotte.

"What's in yours, Mommy?" Kevin asked his mother. Charlotte knew it was time to divert his attention. Her sock bulged with fruit and candies and nuts, but there would be no trinket inside. She couldn't see spending money on herself when finances were so slim, and John, bless his heart, would never think to sneak something into her sock!

"Let's eat before everything gets cold," Charlotte said cheerily, and propped the baby into her high-chair.

"We'll open the others from Grandma and our cousins after breakfast." The chairs clattered against the floor as the family drew them closer to the table. "John, why don't you say the blessing."

"Lord, we thank thee that thou haven't forgotten us this Christmas morning. We thank thee for a warm house, and health, and love. If it be thy will, we ask thee to help us get safely through the snow drifts to the Brown's house for dinner." He opened an eye to peek at Charlotte before adding, "Amen."

Charlotte glanced at John. "Is it questionable?"

"I already did the chores. When we are finished with the packages, I thought I might start the truck and drive down a ways to see what we can expect. I'd rather be the one walking back if the truck gets stuck, than to have these little kids out in it …"

* * *

The baby was done nursing and Kevin was joyfully pulling around Happy, the puppy, in the new little wagon sent to him from Grandma Bush in Kansas, when John entered the house amidst a gust of cold air. "I've put the chains on the truck, and I think we can make it."

"I was thinking you'd make it work!" Charlotte's face beamed. John could see that she had already packed the upside-down cake and the custard pie into one of the brown boxes from which they'd unloaded their Christmas gifts this morning. She covered them with a towel and topped the box with the tea towel she'd embroidered for the Browns. Kevin was proudly bringing his new puppy to show off.

The truck's motor was running and it was warm inside as Charlotte handed bundled Deirdre in for John to hold. She boosted little Kevin, forced into immobility in his heavy snow suit, into the center of the truck seat. She settled herself onto the passenger side of the truck seat, and banged the door shut, straddling the box of cakes and the diaper bag atop it. John handed his wife the wiggling baby girl before he shifted into gear. His baritone rang out in a gusty rendition of "Jingle Bells," and Charlotte and Kevin joined in. Sometimes his voice would grow quiet, and the others' would taper off, too, as they encountered an especially rough spot of snowdrifts. John would shift down and keep the truck steady as it growled through the snowy height.

They had covered most of the three miles when the truck got stuck. John shifted to reverse and hit the gas, only to hear the tires spinning. He stepped on the clutch and slid it back into first gear, but still no forward movement.

"I've got a shovel in the back. I'll see if I can get it out." John opened the truck door and swung out. "Daddy?" Kevin asked with uncertainty.

"It's okay, Kev. Daddy knows how to get our truck out of the snow." Charlotte silently offered a prayer. It would not be good to be stranded out here in the cold with such young ones.

The shovel banged into the bed of the truck and John climbed back in behind the wheel. "Lord, help us move …" Charlotte's voice was barely audible. With the low growl of first gear, the truck moved slowly forward and then picked up enough speed to require a shift into second.

"God helped us, didn't he, Daddy?" Standing in the seat, Kevin put his arm around his father's shoulder and patted it.

"Yes, Kevin. Never forget that Our Lord is ready whenever we ask." John glanced at Charlotte. "I wasn't sure I'd dug it out yet."

The family was singing "I'm Dreaming of a White Christmas" over the roar of the motor as the truck pulled into the lane to the Brown's house. Jack had been out with his tractor and dragged a clear path to the house. He came to the truck and helped Charlotte down as she held the sleeping baby girl, then picked up the fragrant box from the floorboards. Kevin was yelping with pleasure as John perched him onto his shoulder to carry him into the Browns'.

Sophia opened the front door of the tarpaper shack and gestured inside with a "guess what!" expression her face. Charlotte looked past little Georgie hanging onto his mother's skirts, and saw the Christmas tree. It was lit! "You got your electricity finished!" Charlotte's grin matched Sophia's.

"Doesn't seem quite the same without the kerosene lanterns," Jack nudged John. "But I must say, I do like hearing Paul Harvey on the radio over the lunch hour!"

"What did Santa bring you?" Kevin was racing through the living room after Georgie towards his little bedroom. Although this house was still nothing more than a tiny two-bedroom shack, it did have a pitched roof, while the Elwood's one-room home sported only a lean-to roof line. It seemed like a very, very big house to Kevin, with the kitchen set apart from the living room with a partial wall.

The men sat in the living room, swapping tales, amid laughter, of their days in the military.

After placing her sleeping baby in Georgie's crib, Charlotte assisted Sophia in setting the meal on the table. "Oh," Charlotte said as Sophia pulled a bottle of milk from the icebox. "I didn't know if you would use the icebox in the winter. We just keep the cold stored items in a wooden box by the door. Old man winter keeps it plenty cold."

"But, frozen, too." Sophia pointed out. "This way, the milk is just right. Do you think you'll ever get one of those new refrigerators?" With electricity in the house, she could think of lots of possibilities.

"I cannot imagine why," said Charlotte, amazed. Where would she get the money? She and John were hoping to be able to borrow money for seed in the spring, and maybe they would even be able to grow their own hay for the cows for next winter. And even some oats so they could better entice the cows to stand still for the milking.

Sophia mentally counted the steaming dishes on the table and said, "Well, that ought to do it. Let's eat!"

A second call wasn't necessary. The little boys climbed onto the chairs stacked with the thickest books in the house while the adults seated themselves, Jack being the last one, as he had taken time to push in Sophia's chair for her. This all looked a bit ridiculous to John, who had seen how many muscles she'd used to carry that big roaster of turkey with ease.

"Jack," Sophia smiled at her husband, "would you offer our prayer?"

Jack cleared his throat and bowed his dark, freshly brushed thatch of hair. "Dear Father God, thank you for this Christmas day where you gave us Baby Jesus and happy families and good friends and neighbors. Amen."

"And for the food, too." Sophia giggled.

As the friends raised their heads and looked about the food-laden table, John said in a voice suddenly husky, "Well, last year was sure eventful. Here's wishing everyone a very happy 1951!"

CHAPTER 10

Is It Really Spring?

THE SMELL OF burning brush filled the March air. Farmers throughout the area were finishing clearing the sagebrush from their fields. The putt-putt droning of tractors came from all directions. A clear sky showed off the distant mountains.

John leaned on his shovel near a row of burning brush, watching vigilantly that the fire not jump over to the new fence posts that he and Jack had put in together last fall. This definitely felt like headway! He could see clear across the field, now free of scrub cedars and sagebrush. His tractor had been a great help. But, now he squinted and tilted his head as he looked across the field in a different manner, attempting to see where the low spots in the field would be. Irrigation water would be seeking the low spots, and he must be sure his water flow would moisten the entire field uniformly. He couldn't have some areas too wet and some of the field burning up. He would need to use the leveler to rid the field of its lows and highs after he plowed it.

All that working of the soil would get the bothersome cactus turned under, too. Charlotte would probably want to come dig up some tomorrow morning, as she fancied some of the blooms to be "exquisite." She was already showing him the packets of seed she'd bought for planting morning glories around the outer walls of their house. She also had some seeds from her mother's balloon flowers back home; she already knew where she would press them into the earth.

He walked over to his truck, took down a canteen, and took a big swig of water. He used the sleeve of his jacket to wipe his mouth, as he screwed the lid back on. He pulled his lamb's wool collar up around his neck. Boy! These Wyoming spring days were raw! But this sure was a major improvement over that thirty-below-zero day they'd had in early February!

Yes, he would be able to hook up his plow in the morning and begin the work of turning the ground for the first time. His chest grew fuller as he straightened his shoulders. "Just like a darned pioneer," he chuckled aloud.

On his own farmland, Jack was finishing the leveling, using John's leveler on his soon-to-be oat fields. Jack was glad he had finished tilling the ground in time for John to start doing his own leveling. John had laughed at him for getting so eager and trying to till so early in spring. He had told him the ground was so hard it would break his tiller! And, actually, a couple of times earlier he'd found that he couldn't pull up the sagebrush, it just broke off, because the ground was still hard as concrete.

Jack climbed off the tractor and squatted on his haunches, looking over his field to the west, then turning and looking back to the east. He had done it! The ground appeared to be rid of high and low spots. He walked around the leveler, looking for possible need of repair. Even the leveler had come through unscathed!

Back on the tractor, Jack stepped on the clutch and shifted the tractor into gear. The tractor picked up speed as he pulled the leveler down the road, heading for the smoke that rose from where John was working his land. He would have time to say howdy to his friend before heading for home.

Approaching John's, he was careful to keep the tractor far enough from the field to avoid an explosion. John had spotted his approach, and looked over his shoulder at the fire once more before moving in long strides to greet Jack.

"So, you were able to get the leveling done?" John's grin stretched across his weathering face.

"Yes, and I think the irrigation will turn out well enough now. I'm ready to go pick up your disk and finish up the seedbed. I'll be by tomorrow, early, and get it."

John nodded. "It's ready. Don't bother to go to the house to tell us. Just hook onto it."

Jack pointed to John's pant leg, "Looks like you're standing in an ant pile. We might just find out if these are fire ants out here."

"Oh, hell!" John stepped quickly backwards, stomping his boots up and down and swatting at his pants legs. "Guess I owe you one there!" He was smiling in relief.

John strode to the fire and shoveled some dirt on some straying flames. He yelled back to Jack, "I'll be getting to my plowing tomorrow. Some of those winter days weren't good for much but sharpening plow shears! Anyway, looks like you are quite a bit ahead of me getting your fields ready."

Jack's laughter cut across the chilly air. "Sophia says I've been so excited I didn't do anything but toss and turn all night!" He waved to the figure by the burning sagebrush, and started his tractor back down the dirt road towards John's cabin. His mind was running through how he would leave this implement and pick up the next one for tomorrow's work. A jackrabbit hopped quickly from one side of the road to the other, zig-zagging ahead of Jack for a bit before reaching the other side.

CHAPTER II

Faith Versus Fear

"NO, IT'S NOT ready." John shook his head, jostling loose a bee from the brim of his hat. Allowing the fistful of soil to sift through his fingers, he stood from where he had knelt on the ground. "I know it's late April and that would be planting time in Oklahoma, but, Jack, this is Wyoming! It got down to forty below zero this winter! The topsoil still has ice crystals in it. Besides, you know what the Farmer's Almanac says. It can freeze until May fifteenth."

Jack slowly let the dirt fall from his hand, too. His brows drew down over his blue eyes. "I guess you're right. Another week might make the difference. I'm going to plant oats. Seed prices are pretty good for oats right now."

"I have the grain drill all ready, checked it out already," John told his friend, as he tugged his collar up against the chilly morning breeze. "Don't come to the house and ask. Just drive in and hitch up. We'll know it's you. Just make sure all is clean for my seed when it comes back."

"So. You are wanting to plant alfalfa, right?" Jack squinted against the sun that shone brightly in spite of the chill in the air. "What about the aphids? I read in the Farm News that aphids have been heading our way."

"You know what, Jack? God made all types of critters, and if we stay huddled in fear of their attack, we won't plant anything. Why, you and I wouldn't even be out here. We'd be too afraid of the rattlers."

"I've only seen one so far," Jack nodded. "I had my shovel with me. I chopped his head right off. Kept the rattle. Think I'm going to make me a collection of them."

"Don't know as the women are ready to see any rattler collection just yet!" John's laughter rang out across the field. "Why, Charlotte had a fit about that little nest of mice we found in her mother's tablecloth box! I told her they're just cold and will be moseying out when the warmer weather comes."

"Well, you killed them, didn't you?" Jack was smiling broadly, too.

"Sure. Put them in a bag and threw them into the canal. But it made Kevin cry. He liked the babies, all pink and all ... I think that boy of mine needs a real dog soon. He seems to have a real craving for a living thing of his own."

"I've got a magazine with everything from different breeds of dogs to baby chicks you can order. I'll lend it to you." Jack patted John on the shoulder.

As the two men headed for their vehicles parked alongside the dirt road, they turned towards the sound of an approaching motor. It was the mail carrier, waving as he passed them by, to keep his schedule while dropping off the much-prized letters.

"We sure do get excited over the mail at our house," John told Jack. "Is your wife doing okay without any phones out here to call her mother?"

"I know what you mean. Sometimes I also feel so danged glad to see that mail car that I think I'll run out and bark at it! We don't even think about telephones anymore, John. The baby doing okay?"

"Yeah. And we have a new one in the oven, again."

Jack stopped in amazement and clapped one hand to the side of his head. "Whoa! Now, I'll never hear the end of it with Sophia. All I hear from her is that Georgie needs someone to play with. She might be right. But, it's so far to the doctor and all, forty-five miles to Riverton. I guess I just worry about her out here in this no-man's land."

"This is our life," John said in a husky voice. "The Good Lord helped us draw these portions of land. He gave us good women to love. And, I think He's given us right good neighbors, too! So, if the Good Lord can do all that, why shouldn't we trust Him to help us get the women to the hospital for babies?"

Jack swallowed, ducked his head, and came back up with a smile. "Guess I'd better get home and start work on another kind of crop, huh?"

John was still smiling when he drove his truck into the yard of his farmstead. He gazed about him. He looked at the neat row of fence posts that surrounded his cow corral. He looked at the cattle shed, rough-hewn, but very sturdy. And the house looked so lived-in already, with the curtains hanging behind the windows. And, there, that was the real pride! The beginning of a real three-bedroom house. Well, maybe it just looked like piles of lumber and bags of concrete under the tarp for now. But he and Charlotte had spent many a night poring over house plans and finally settled on this one. She wanted the big front-room picture window to overlook the road. And he'd placed the house strategically upwind to avoid as much as possible the scent from the barn. Phew! Some of those older farms he drove past on a Sunday afternoon sure did stink from their cows and pigs. Bacon only smelled so good when still on the hoof. Yes, John could see the sure progress that had come along in the year since he first got out here to his land.

John sat for a bit in the truck, seeing the dirt and sagebrush all about him, the cactus poking up from time to time. But, now there were areas that were smooth and free of the cactus and sagebrush, where he had tilled the land and turned it into a farm. He followed the flight of an eagle overhead and saw it disappear into the distance, where the horizon was rimmed all around by the purple mountain range.

Soon, it would be warm enough for fly fishing and picnicking in those mountains on Sunday afternoons. Charlotte would want to invite as many friends as they could fit onto the benches in the back of the truck. That girl knew how to make fun happen! And she would insist on church and Sunday fun, not Sunday work in the fields.

He pulled off his hat and ran his hand through his brush of hair. With the weather starting to break, he'd have to be sure that Kevin understood never, never to go near the canals and ditches around the farm. It had been fun on some of the mildest winter afternoons to take the tyke hiking and help him pick up the bison horns and collect old arrowheads from when Indians had fought on these plains. But, the water was now coursing through those canals and a child could drown very quickly.

Still, he remembered his words to Jack, and the trust in his Good Lord brought back his smile as he stomped the dirt from his boots before entering his little house.

"Daddy! Daddy!" Kevin ran to throw himself at his father. "Look, Di Dee is trying to crawl!" Already, the boy was such a helper for his little sister. John knew there were times when Charlotte was visiting the outhouse or bringing in wood, and their son was good at watching his sister in the jumpy seat while the grownups were busy. But, wow. Soon the boy would be five. Kevin's birthday! That would be a good time to start looking through Jack's animal magazine. Collies make good dogs for boys.

Charlotte swooped up Deirdre, clothed in overhauls to keep her knees from splinters on the floor, and came over to give John a peck of a kiss. They would never be more romantic in front of the kids. Just wouldn't be proper.

Her blue bandanna matched her blue eyes and she had the glow of early pregnancy about her. "You okay?" he asked, keeping the real topic of his question a secret from the inquisitive boy.

"Yes, no more early morning up-chucks. Honey, I've been thinking. Kevin's been trying not to suck his thumb anymore." Charlotte nodded her head approvingly towards Kevin, her eyes crinkling in a smile at him. "Seems to me it could be a special birthday when he turns five if he is all done sucking his thumb by then."

The tow-headed child's face lit proudly and he quickly thrust into his pocket the traitor hand with the wrinkled thumb that had been creeping towards his pink mouth.

"Sounds like a pretty big boy now," John agreed, grinning at the little boy who looked up at him so hopefully.

CHAPTER 12

Frills

THE JUNE SUN beat down on Henry's already reddened neck as he hunched forward to caulk the chink between yet another set of logs. Who would have thought it would take so long for him to build his Flora this little cabin! It hadn't helped that he couldn't get away from his mining job until March. Good thing he'd been able to slip away to take the train to Pennsylvania for those two days over Christmas! Flora had looked so lovely, with her black bouncy curls gathered up on the back of her head and that red lipstick! No wonder they had gotten a new baby started.

That Flora! Her letters were all full of worrying about losing her figure. It sounded like her pregnancy was really going well, though. He wished he was there to take Flora to the doctor appointments. Flora's dad understands a young husband needing to prepare a home for his bride, but Flora's mother could be darned uppity, and was probably filling her head with stories of dread about pioneering.

Henry straightened and rubbed his back. The interior's caulking was done. He would Sheetrock two walls of the living room tomorrow. He would Sheetrock the wall behind the kitchen sink. Then, he could paint all the other interior log walls. He guessed he would choose a sea green paint. That would set off Flora's dark hair quite beautifully. He had worked hard on the linoleum, probably spending more time than he ought. But, he'd wanted to cut in that diamond design into the center of the kitchen. Everyone knew that loving started in the kitchen.

There was just time before dark, if he really lengthened his stride, to take a walk through the garden and see how the corn and squash were doing. He had better move the pipes and see if he could moisten some of the other rows tomorrow. Wyoming summers sure were dry!

A whippoorwill cried out, "whip-poor-will, whip-poor-will," as Henry strode—carefully watching where he stepped—the twelve hundred feet over to the garden. He would not soon forget the snake he'd seen on this very ground, which was being beaten into a path. The rattler had raised its head a bit to peer at him as Henry jerked to a stop, his breath drawn in. He'd remained very still, and the snake had finally lowered its head, with flicking tongue. He had thought he might wet himself with relief when it slithered away out of sight. He had omitted this event from his letter to Flora, but was now ever so watchful in walking, in picking up a board, or in sitting upon a rock to eat his sandwich.

After he had dammed the ditch that carried the water to his garden, Henry moved the pipes so that tomorrow he could open the water gate to water several other rows. He examined the squash and the corn. "Corn is supposed to be knee high by the Fourth of July," he muttered to himself. It would have to grow some to get there in the next few weeks. He would get some tomato plants from Riverton and plant them this week, too. It would be good to get them started before he brought Flora out. Jack Brown had offered to water his garden while he was back East fetching Flora. That's right kind of Jack, as late July would be an extremely busy time for farmers around here.

Henry's brother and dad were already busy gathering up his things from the equipment shed, and helping Flora to pack the things she would not need right at the last. They had helped him locate a flat car that would bring these items out on the railroad when it was time to move here. His brother, Grover, had volunteered for the military but was colorblind and had flat feet and never got to go to the war. Once again Grover, the college student, was watching his younger brother engage in a lifestyle that looked very much like high adventure. Maybe when he finished his lawyer school, he would decide to come live in Riverton, Wyoming, or Lander, and have an adventure of his own! It would be nice to have some family around.

The radishes were up nicely now, and that over there must be the lettuce. When the Browns had come by, and he'd shown them his garden, Sophia had told him that she half buries the empty seed packets at the ends of the rows so she can remember what is planted where. That would have been a good idea! Well, next time. But, maybe it will be Flora planting them next year.

Henry detoured to the outhouse on his way back into the house. He washed his hands and got a drink of water from the faucet inside the roughed-in kitchen. Only a bit more and he would be ready to hook up the electricity to the pole, too. But, for now, he got down the kerosene lantern and turned up its wick and struck a match to light it. He opened the icebox and checked the ice block before getting out a beer. Hmmm. Last one. Good thing he'd bought a case last time in Riverton. A six-pack used to do him a week, now it seems it is gone in two or three days. He found the bottle opener on the sawhorse and popped it open. The first gulp was long and hard, and Henry sat down heavily in his only chair as the familiar heat went down his throat and spread through his body and into his head.

He closed his eyes and listened. The June bugs were snapping against the door. Crickets were chirping outside. Or drat, had one gotten inside again? He could hear the putt-putt-putt of a John Deere tractor heading home from the fields. That would be John Elwood. John was sure a decent fellow. It had been good of him to tack back down his tarpaper when it started coming off the roof last winter. No worries about that sort of thing now, with the blue shingles Henry had since nailed carefully into place.

Some might have thought it a waste of time for him to be putting down a brick path to the house, but they didn't know his Flora! Only he knew of the certain niceties that could help swing her attitude toward the kind of style she was being introduced to here in the prairie life of Wyoming!

He ought to get up and finish painting the cupboards he'd built for the kitchen. That'd mean lighting another lamp. What? The beer already finished? Better have another. Oops. He'd forgotten to get some bottles from the case and place them in the icebox. He'd do that now, and maybe a warm beer wouldn't be so bad in the meanwhile.

CHAPTER 13

Settling Things

"**B**UT WE ALREADY borrowed money for seed this spring, John." Charlotte's forehead was creased with worry. The couple stood at a distance from where Kevin played with his little metal truck on the intricate dirt roads he had fashioned. Deirdre's little legs were tugging her little blue metal "walker" in a circle on the ground nearby. Charlotte had to keep her eye out for that one, or she would snag a wheel on a rock and tip the walker.

Charlotte knew that this matter was of utmost importance, for John had come striding into the house before he had completed all his irrigating for the day. He usually didn't show up until noon for dinner, which she would have on the table by the stroke of twelve. John didn't carry a watch, but his stomach always guided him home for a noon dinner break.

John shifted his shovel from where it perched over his shoulder, and he put it to the ground and leaned on it. "Hon, that money's long gone. You wrote the checks yourself. We still seem to be eating. You find something to feed us, even though the garden isn't putting out much yet. I see we've used up all the canning from last fall. But right now, we have the bill to pay for filling the gasoline tank, and it's time to order some more water. We have to have water or these crops will dry up in no time."

Charlotte sighed and rubbed her hands down the sides of her yellow, summer polka dot skirt. Her ruffled yellow maternity smock hung over her growing abdomen. She tugged at the blond curl that kept creeping over her left eye. "I just grow afraid that, at harvest, we will not clear enough to do anything but make the loan payments. And, I know we are praying for a good crop and it does look like a good one is coming, but I know something could happen to keep us from getting it from the fields, and then how would we even pay the loan, let alone eat?"

John was right, there was always something to eat. Her mother had taught her how to make a meal stretch, having raised Charlotte during the Depression. But she had a baby inside to think of. She could deal with just a glass of milk and bread mushed up in it for dinner when there weren't enough servings of hash potatoes and hamburger meat to go around. So far, John seemed to believe her that it was her preference to eat the bread and milk, and to not perceive it was her way of making sure the others had their share. But, with a growing fetus, it was a different story. This child inside had to have his nutrients, too.

Charlotte knew it would take a harvest to buy more provisions, but it was hard to think of getting so far into debt so soon.

"John, can we pray about it tonight, and let the Lord lead us in this?" John heaved a breath, took off his sweat-stained, felt Western hat and ran a hand through his brown hair. He nodded and put his shovel back over his shoulder as he headed back to the fields. The canvas rolls still lay where he'd dropped them at the end of the garden. He stopped and picked them up on his way. They would be needed to dam the water from the rows of alfalfa that were already refreshed, turning the flow toward some parched ones.

Charlotte pulled Deirdre from the "walker" and picked up the wheeled carrier with the other hand. "Kevie, don't leave where you are until you come into the house. If you see a snake, don't move but yell really loud, so I can come kill it. You tell Mommy if you need me to go with you to the outhouse."

Charlotte knew he was nearly five and really quite big now, and John had said she should let him go to the outhouse alone so he would feel brave in this harsh country, but she was so fearful that these rattlers around here might get her child.

"Mommy! What is that?" Charlotte could tell that Kevin's voice was happily excited, not worried. Good. Wouldn't be a snake, then. Charlotte had just reached the door with her daughter. She placed the walker on the doorstep and turned to hurry back towards Kevin. She slowed as she approached, because she could see his face was quite animated, his finger pointing towards a heap of earth near a sagebrush clump that was swaying slightly in the breeze.

Charlotte picked up a nearby rake in the event she might need to impale some varmint. Deirdre tried to pull at its handle as her mother balanced the rake and the child.

"There! There. Under the sagebrush. Is it a giant mouse?" Kevin's voice was shrill.

As Charlotte approached the bush, a gray creature scurried out and disappeared. Whew! It was quite sizeable. Charlotte moved her rake around in the area from which he'd come. Well, look at that! In what appeared to be his nest, the creature had placed a bright pink piece of celluloid from Deirdre's broken doll. And there was a piece of blue glistening glass, and here was the piece of turquoise in its silver mounting that had fallen from her key chain last month. She had looked and looked for that. The rat must have better eyes than she.

"Kevin, come see!" Charlotte called to the little boy. He leaped to his feet and his little boots pumped to hurry to his mother's side, already adept at side-stepping the cactus on the way. "See all these pretties? That was a pack rat. He's named 'pack rat' because he loves pretties just like we do, and he packs them off to his nest. If we lose something new, we might want to come see if he has found it for us. Right now, I am going to take back the piece to my key chain. I hope he won't be so upset with my stirring in his nest that he won't come back and make it home. It's probably good I still have my gloves on."

"Look, Di Dee." Kevin was always so good to include his baby sister in his discoveries. "It's just a nice pack rat. He won't hurt us. He seems to be scared of us!"

Charlotte braced the rake against her middle and patted the little boy's shoulder. "Okay, son. Back to making your roads. We probably need to leave this nest alone or the pack rat won't ever come back. I wonder where he's hiding so that he can watch us right now."

Kevin looked around, as though to glimpse the rat again, on his way back to his road-building project. Charlotte headed for the door of the cabin once again. She had time to hem a few more canvas dams and maybe even to pin a pattern on the newly laundered cotton flour sack. She had chosen this particular fifty-pound bag of flour because of the red rose buds scattered over the cotton bag. She'd known then that this would make a very sweet dress for Deirdre. And she knew just what she'd do with her own old blouse that couldn't bear another patch. She would rip the red rickrack from that blouse and trim the baby's little dress. The rest of the blouse would make some rags for when she resumed her menstrual periods. This freedom from such mess was a real blessing of being pregnant. She wondered if the other ladies on the homestead felt the same way when pregnant. But, of course, one would never speak of such things. She'd not be speaking of the pregnancy either;

the others would start to mention it when it began to look as though the baby would arrive soon.

Charlotte knew it was good she'd had the "work before play" upbringing, or she'd be setting aside those dull canvas dams and starting her daughter's dress right now.

First, she went to the sink and pulled down the pink cup to draw a drink of water for the wiggling child. "Dink, dink!" Deirdre approved.

When the little girl had finished her drink, with loud, slurping sounds, Charlotte carefully scooted that cup to the back of the counter. She grasped a metal blue glass for a drink of water for herself. Everyone had their own glass in this family. She would wash them at the end of the day so that each day brought a fresh start to their glasses. John had seemed amazed at her insistence upon this, but Charlotte knew enough about germs to know this would keep her family healthier than sharing drinking containers like he'd been used to. Why, John had grown up with a number of brothers and they'd all drunk from a mutual dipper in the pail of water. John still had a left-over habit from those days. Even though it was his own clean glass and he was filling it from running water out of the faucet, he would half fill the glass, swish it around, and then pour it out abruptly, before filling it again with water he then would drink. Apparently, his brothers and he had thought that kind of treatment to the water dipper had cleaned the former brother's saliva from it! My, she was glad to be living in these modern times!

She smiled as she settled Deirdre on the floor with half a dozen wooden blocks, and showed her how to stack them. Deirdre quickly knocked them down, laughing, and looked at her mother to stack them again.

"Not me. You do it, Deirdre, you stack them!" Charlotte laughed and stood up, taking the stack of books from her sewing machine cabinet. In a little house like this, every piece of furniture served several purposes. Now that it was no longer a bookcase, she flipped the top of the sewing machine cabinet open and placed the pedal on the floor underneath it, plugging her machine into an electric wall plate.

Charlotte pulled the folded white canvas from where it had been placed atop the pile of boxes along the wall. She used the yardstick to measure the canvas she had laid out on the kitchen table. It had to be long enough to make a place for the board John would saw off to insert in the larger hem. She pulled a kitchen chair over in front of the sewing machine and seated herself. Carefully pulling the thread to the left of the presser foot, she released the presser foot onto the doubled-over canvas that would form the bottom hem. Her foot pressed the lever on the floor and the heavy needle began to make its way through the fabric. She'd known when John told her they would be using canvas for dams that if she didn't hem each raw piece of the material, it would soon fray out. They would have to use their dams again and again. This was just one of the ways they could keep saving precious pennies.

Oops. Deirdre's chirping had quieted, and as Charlotte glanced towards her, she saw that the child had crawled to the diaper pail and was standing up against it. Charlotte didn't think she could tip it over, or get the lid off, but she'd better place her alongside the bunk bed to do her practice walking. Rising, the young woman went to lift the chubby child and carry her to stand alongside the bed. She placed a cloth book about shapes on the bedspread to entice Deirdre further. "See. See the pretty ball on this page. And here is a square. It is shaped like the window!" Deirdre held the side of the bed as she patted the page of the book. She suddenly bent her head and kissed the page. Charlotte laughed and rubbed the baby's back before heading back to her sewing.

Maybe she wouldn't get to the flour sack this morning. Looked like she'd barely get two more dams finished before she had to fold up the machine in order to prepare the noon dinner. It would be handier to leave the sewing machine out, but then the baby might get her finger under the needle.

Deirdre was whimpering and Charlotte rose to see what was happening. The baby wasn't at the side of the bed anymore but now had picked up a piece of firewood near the black stove. "Good grief, Deirdre!" The child had poked herself with a nail poking from the wood, but it didn't look too bad. Charlotte kissed the plump hand near the wound and the whimpering stopped. Her mother carried the toddler to the kitchen sink and turned the faucet onto it. Then, she reached up to a cabinet hanging above the sink and got out a bottle of

Merthiolate. She held the little hand over the sink as she gently poured a small amount of the reddish orange medicine over the scratch on the child's hand. Deirdre pulled her hand from her mother's. She made a sound, and Charlotte understood because the ingredients that killed the germs did burn one's wound.

Carefully putting the medication back in the cabinet, and washing the sink so it wouldn't stain, Charlotte carried the child to her crib and changed her diaper. She placed Deirdre on the floor again with her teddy bear and headed to the cabinets to fix the noon meal. Maybe there would be one ripe enough tomato. She swooped up the child and went out to the garden. Yes, this is the one she'd had her eye on. She got to it before John had. John liked to come home in the evening and check out the garden for ripe treats, brushing them on his pants leg before trying out the vegetables. Hmmm ... if she pulled an onion, it would be small but tasty in little slivers on the salad. The loose-leaf lettuce could be trimmed now to finish out the salad.

Charlotte talked with the baby as she strode over to where Kevin appeared to be making a tunnel in his dirt pile. "Let me carry these to the house, Kevie, and I'll walk to the outhouse with you. You can hold Deirdre while Mommy uses the outhouse, too." Kevin nodded, patting his dirt into place.

When she had placed the vegetables inside the house, Charlotte headed onto the path leading to the outhouse. "Come on, Kevin," she called.

Kevin ran to join his mother, quickly moving ahead of her on the path. "I want to go first." Charlotte agreed, but stepped into the outhouse with him, holding her breath against the familiar smell. Her glance took in the wooden bench with the hole in the center. No fresh spider webs had been spun across it. She nonchalantly glanced down into the depths of the hole. John thought her very silly in looking down there, but she had carried a secret fear from her own childhood that a snake might lie in wait to bite her bottom when she sat down.

As Kevin lowered his britches and she helped him scoot up onto the seat, he pointed to the spiders busy building their webs in the corners of the little building. "Are those black widows, Mommy?"

Charlotte tried to subdue her shudder and cautioned him, "Just don't ever touch them, or back into them, and we won't have to know."

She watchfully shook out the catalogue lying on the bench near Kevin, and told him to pull out two pages. "I know, I know," he said tolerantly, "I never need more than two pages to wipe." As long as those Christmas catalogues from J. C. Penney and Montgomery Wards kept coming, they'd not have to resort to corn cobs like some of the neighbors told her they did.

"Nope. And no-no, to you, too, young lady." Charlotte quickly grasped Deirdre's reaching hand and kept it from the spider web in the corner, and stepped out into the welcome fresh air.

Kevin got himself down from the seat and pulled up his clothes. He stepped out and reached for his little sister.

"Okay, Deirdre. I'm going to hold you while Mommy goes potty."

Charlotte stepped up into the outhouse and closed the door. John had fashioned it so that there was a piece of wood that would twist to close it shut from the inside. And there was an identical chunk of wood on the outside that they used to keep it closed from the exterior. That was very nice in the winter, when it kept snow from blowing inside. Kevin had only once turned the handle and locked her inside while she was using the outhouse. She'd hollered at him until he opened it, and she'd used the yardstick on him to teach him a lesson he wouldn't forget!

They had finished outdoors and went into the house to wash their hands. This was another thing upon which Charlotte insisted. There was a lot of dirt in this world of theirs and it was pointless to wash one's hands all the time. But after a visit to that smelly outhouse, it was a MUST! They used the bar of soap lying beside the kitchen sink. It was one of seven yet left that Charlotte's mother had made before the Elwoods moved out here to Wyoming. Inside was hidden a trinket, maybe a special button, that one only got to by using the soap until it was gone. It definitely kept Kevin interested in washing his hands.

Now, let's see. There was enough ham left for a small portion for each of them, with Deirdre's being cut and mashed into tiny morsels. And there was just time to dice three potatoes and set them on the stove to boil, so there could be mashed potatoes. Charlotte would cook a pudding mix and make butterscotch pudding for dessert, and pour some of the cow's thick cream over the top.

Charlotte was so glad they'd brought the milk separator with them. Turning the handle separated the milk from the thick cream. Charlotte churned their butter, and it could be kept in the well pit for quite a spell before it went rancid.

John was stomping his boots outside the door, and Kevin raced to open it with a gleeful, "Daddy! Daddy!" One would think he'd been gone for days.

"Smells good in here," said John, as he breathed in the smells of butterscotch and hot potatoes. "Where's the bread?"

Charlotte smiled. He wouldn't notice if everything on the table was the same color, although she always tried to have her chipped plates of food have some different colors on them. But he would always notice if she forgot the bread or the salt and pepper.

John tossed his hat on the floor under his chair and sat down. "Isn't it time for Paul Harvey?" He knew how to turn on the radio, too, but somehow it had become part of Charlotte's work of dinner preparations to turn Paul Harvey on for them all to enjoy during the midday meal.

Charlotte placed Deirdre in her high-chair, Kevin crawled onto the bench his daddy had made while he lived here that summer by himself, and the two adults pulled the two kitchen chairs to seat themselves. "Hello, everyone. This is Paul Harvey," the familiar voice rang out. "Well, Angel and I have celebrated another anniversary ..."

Charlotte smiled at John. It seemed that Paul and Angel Harvey were moving along with their marriage at about the same pace as the Elwoods. This was the time during the meal when no one talked. Even Deirdre was especially busy eating her bites of meat. It was just too much fun hearing the good news in which only Paul Harvey specialized.

When Paul Harvey had ended his newscast with his familiar, "Paul Harvey, good day!" Charlotte asked John about his morning.

"Well, I saw a rattler today. It struck me in the rubber hip-boot. I got its head chopped off, and I have a new set of fine rattles now."

Charlotte didn't look as thrilled as Kevin did. "Really, Daddy, can I rattle them?"

Charlotte interrupted, "Is it safe for him to touch them, John? Can he get poison from them?"

John's laugh rumbled. "The snake didn't have poison in his tail end, Charlotte. The poison is only through his fangs. Those are like teeth, Kevin. Sure, when we are finished here, I'll get out the old rattle and let you shake it."

"Well, meanwhile, we got a letter from my mother today. Would you like to hear it?" Charlotte had the envelope lying by her plate. This was the time they usually shared news from back home.

She poured a little more milk in Deirdre's cup and opened the letter and began to read:

"Dear Charlotte, John, and kids: It is a nice summer day here in Kansas City, Kansas, and I wonder if the weather is nice there, too. You say it hardly ever rains, so I guess chances are, it is pretty nice there, too, today. Your sister Zelda had her baby yesterday. Jim called to tell me about it after it was born. She had another girl, twenty-one inches long and eight pounds, ten ounces. Seems she has bigger babies than you. Maybe it is because you work so hard before they come."

Charlotte glanced at her husband. They both knew that John's mother-in-law loved him, but she also was resentful that he had trotted her daughter off to this far-away, unbroken prairie land. They hadn't told Mama yet that there was another baby on the way here. There'd be time enough for that.

"Stephen was in a wreck. I don't know how it happened. He was going down Main Street towards the lumberyard, and he says the car just came out of nowhere. It ran into his passenger side and jostled him around quite a bit. His head hit the window glass on his side of the car, and his neck hurts some. We didn't take him to the doctor, as he insisted it wasn't that bad. I do wonder though if it did more than dent in the door and side of the car. It feels like the tires slip when I turn the steering column."

John snorted, "Probably needs her linkage adjusted. Who ever heard of the tires slipping when you turn the steering wheel."

Charlotte resumed reading, her eyes twinkling. "You know Stephen is always getting these hare-brained notions. He thinks he might just come out and see you all this fall and do some pheasant hunting while he is there."

Charlotte's eyes met John's. "Oh, it would be swell to see my brother. And pheasants make good eating. That would be just great. I'd put him up in the top bunk over Kevin."

John was getting restless. His water needed tending.

"The roses are pretty just now. I'd love to be able to pick one and bring it over to you. But, I'd better close and get this in the mail. Can you believe the postage costs three cents for a stamp now? Much love, Mom."

Kevin was examining the high-priced postage stamp as John rose to retrieve his hat from beneath the chair. "Better get back out there. Time's a wastin'. Oh, dang! I dropped puddin' in my hat."

Charlotte's head tilted back with laugher, but it was Kevin who couldn't stop laughing. He jumped off the bench and ran to look inside his dad's hat. "You going to eat it, Daddy?"

John ruffled the child's hair. "No. We aren't that hungry yet." He got the dishrag from the sink and wiped out the hat before slapping it onto his head. Charlotte gave him a hug before turning to get the little girl from her high-chair. Deirdre was weaving forward and then to the side, her eyes closed and a finger twirling in her curls. "Better put this one to bed before she hits her head on the high-chair tray."

As his wife was carrying the baby to her crib, John put his hand in his pants pocket and pulled out the unfortunate snake's rattle. Kevin reached his hand tentatively, but his father encouraged him, "Go ahead. Pick it up and shake it."

Kevin did, and the "trrrr" sound of the rattles had its own distinct sound. "That is what a rattlesnake sounds like, Kevin. He shakes the rattle to warn you that he's about to strike. And he has poison in his mouth. If he strikes, it's not good."

The little boy was almost reverent in his study of the rattle. "Go ahead. Put it there on the windowsill," John said. "That's where we'll put the others I bring, too."

"Others?" Charlotte shivered.

John went to the sink and got his own green metal glass down. He turned on the spigot and ran water into the glass. Then, he swished it in his customary way, hurling the water out into the sink abruptly. He filled the glass anew and drank deeply.

"I'll be taking one of these new dams you made, me, Charlotte." The door swung shut behind John. He sat on the doorstep to pull on his hip-boots. He bent down and peered at the two new indentations. Those fangs were sharp!

As he made sure his flannel gloves were in his hip pocket, he stood, swinging the shovel over his shoulder. His steps were long as he headed back to the field. You could tell a lot about a man from the way he walked. Any little short prissy steps would say a guy wasn't much of a man.

He walked past the rows of little trees that would one day be a windbreak from the cold northern winds. He pushed his shovel into the ground beside them. They didn't need watering again quite yet. He could see new green sprigs on the trees. The little sticks from last fall had done pretty well, really.

John whistled as he reached the fence. A nice strong fence. He hadn't resorted to manual posthole diggers like he'd seen one of the neighbors trying to maneuver. He had put the posthole auger on the tractor and that had saved a lot of time. He and Jack had helped each other with their fences, using the auger and the other's tractor to stretch the wire taut. Then, the staples had been driven in with their hammers. He made sure he was next to the pole as he grasped the wire between the barbs and climbed up over the tallest strand. He enjoyed his walk to where he needed to change the water. There were birds to see, yellow cactus blooming, and even some pink wild primrose. And, it looked like the prairie dogs had built themselves a little city over there by the little road he'd started. When they got Kevin's dog, it would probably have fun trying to catch them.

He approached the area that was hard and dry, with the soil cracking on top. The alfalfa plants looked droopy. He had gotten around to watering them just in time! He went to the end of the row and pulled up the water dam across the little ditch.

He used his shovel to make the groove into the next six rows a bit cleaner. Then he went to the ditch beside the tenth corrugation and stooped to settle in the new dam. He used Charlotte's fresh one. With deft motions, he dug mud from near the dam and tamped it onto the canvas, making sure it would hold against the flow of water. Now the water would have more force as it pushed down the six new rows he'd opened. He carried the used dam back to where he had watered already and used it to plug the pathway to the alfalfa plants that were already standing tall.

What was that peeping sound? Oh, look! A little baby pheasant near his watering ditch. It might fall in and drown. He'd just as well take it home and see if Charlotte and Kevin could keep it alive. Would be good for Kevin to get some practice looking after a living thing. He carefully slipped the bird into his shirt pocket, the one his shovel arm wouldn't rest against.

Yes, the crop did look good. If he let some of it dry out in another week, he thought he could get in and cut some hay on just a portion of the field. Two cuttings could be gotten out here, maybe three in a better year. But two would get him enough bales to keep two cows going for the winter. Mostly, he wanted this field to ripen and produce the little curling seeds of alfalfa. The price per bushel was darned good right now.

It appeared to be nearing four o'clock as John stepped back onto his doorstep. There'd be time to get another drink of water and then go out and milk the cows.

"Daddy!" Kevin looked up from where he was building towers from blocks on the floor with Deirdre. "Mommy says this is Rapunzel's Tower!"

"Where is Mommy?"

"She's at the outhouse. She said her tummy was hurting."

"Kev, my boy, keep watching your sister. I'll be back inside in just a minute."

John's quick steps were determined as he approached the outhouse.

"Charlotte, you in there? Are you okay, Hon?"

Charlotte swung the door open on the smelly little hut. She sat inside, laughing. "Yes. Why do you ask?"

"Kevin said you had a stomach ache."

"Sorry I worried you. That's what I get for exaggerating. He didn't want to watch Deirdre and I knew it would take me awhile here. I got him to take pity on me by saying my tummy hurt."

"Hmmm." John smiled at her and then headed back to the house.

"Kevin," he said, bending over the little boy, "what do you guess is in Daddy's pocket?"

The child stood and pulled his hand back to smack the pocket. John caught his arm in time. "No. No. You must be gentle. I have a surprise for you in here. What do you think it is?"

Kevin wrinkled his face in thought. "A new arrowhead?" he ventured.

"No. Do you give up?" John smiled and waved to Deirdre, too.

"Show me, show me," the child begged, pulling at his father's hand.

John went to the kitchen chair and sat down. He looked down at his pocket as he carefully placed a thumb and two fingers inside it. Something was cheeping inside there! When his dad's hand came out of the pocket, it held a tiny baby bird.

"It is a pheasant, Kevin. If it grows up, it will be nearly as big as a grown chicken. I saved it from falling into the water. Maybe you and Mommy can take care of it and see if you can help it grow up big."

"Is it a boy?" Kevin peered closely at the bird, and touched its soft, light brown down.

"I don't know, Kev. Hold out your hands and I'll let you hold him. Scoop your hands together." John set the quivering bird into the plump little hands.

"Oh … no, Deirdre. You can't squeeze him. You are too little."

The little girl had crawled quickly to his side, and had pulled up against John's knee. She bent her head and tried to kiss the baby pheasant.

Charlotte pushed open the door. "What's all the excitement?"

"It's a baby pheasant!" Kevin called out importantly. "Daddy brought him home for you and me to take care of. He saved it from falling into the water."

"Well, now, let's see, little pheasant. Hmmm … I think I know just the right box for you." Charlotte went to the draped-off corner near her bed and pulled out a shoebox. "We'll put one of our old towels in it and make it a nice warm bed. I'll bet Daddy will chew up a worm for its supper, too."

John grinned over her head, "Maybe you could cook him up a couple of macaronis? I must get out there and milk the cows now."

As he picked up the clean milk pail from behind the door, he found himself whistling. "The more you hug and kiss the girls, the more they want to marry." He wasn't sure what he'd done to deserve to be this happy, but he was feeling mighty content with his life just now.

He sure hoped the time after their prayer tonight went as well as the rest of the day had!

CHAPTER 14

Womenfolk

SOPHIA DEFTLY PULLED the clothespin from the bag hanging on the line and pinned the corner of the wet towel to the towel next to it. Pinning the last corner to the high wire, she picked up the basket and cocked her head to listen before she headed back to the house. The sounds of the summer morning were now growing familiar to her. She could hear the putt-putt of a tractor in the distance, where Jack was helping John get some hay in from the field. And, there was the sound of the water pouring over its drops in the lateral ditch. Frogs were having their singing competition as well. One could almost say it sounded like home!

Sophia glanced towards the swing where Georgie was practicing pumping, his little legs going out and then knees bent back. His head was thrown back, and it appeared he might have his eyes closed, no doubt imagining himself flying high as an eagle.

As she stepped on the stones from which Jack had fashioned a path to the house, she could see a grasshopper leap ahead of her step. She was glad they were not seeing a whole lot of the insects. While it seemed to be normal in this dry country to see an occasional grasshopper, she knew hoppers could descend upon crops in droves and clean out an entire harvest.

She swung open the door to the house and entered, leaving the door open, but the screen door snapped shut to keep out the flies. At that, a couple had entered when she had. She dropped the basket and pulled the fly-swatter from a nail on the end of the kitchen counter. She meant business when she went after those flies, smacking them a death-blow and then scooping them up on the end of the swatter to deposit in the trashcan.

She went to the window, pulling aside the curtain to better see Georgie. He was still playing on the swing. He seemed very obedient and sincere in his promises to stay away from the ditches of water, but she kept a good eye out for him. She was always expecting to hear on the radio that a child had drowned in one of the ditches, or even a canal.

Radio! She smiled to herself, recalling how she and Jack had laughed aloud this morning when a new broadcaster had been announcing the price of crop seeds and animals. He had called a sheep ewe an "ee-wee!" It had taken them a moment to even figure out what he had been trying to say!

Jack would be a bit later than usual getting home tonight because he would take a detour and go by the Zanders'. Jack had been watering their garden. He said it was coming along. He had picked some tomatoes from it and told Sophia they should eat them if they were spoiling before Henry got back. Sophia figured she'd just can them and give them to the Zanders that way instead.

Henry had gone back East to fetch his wife and belongings, so they could finally make their home here. It seemed to Jack and her that Henry had taken an unusual length of time to get things ready for the move. But maybe Jack was right when he said he suspects Henry is working on a drinking problem. He said he'd stumbled upon a big pile of beer bottles where it looked as though Henry had tried to bury them.

This would be rugged country for a drunkard. Probably a good thing that pretty Flora would be joining him here to keep an eye on him. Maybe he wouldn't drink so much if he were less lonely. Even the pastor had said, "It's not good for man to be alone."

Sophia cast an eye around her kitchen, tugging a towel hanging from the oven door into a neater fold. She picked up a dusting rag and moved into the living room and began to rub it across the top of the coffee table and the sewing machine cabinet. Today was Club day and she wanted to make it especially nice. That pleasant lady from the County Extension Office in Riverton had visited, and told her how much nicer it is in a Homestead project if the women get together once a month for a Club meeting. She would be the first hostess. She had prepared a nice apple crunch dessert to serve at the end. The hardest part had been figuring out the names of all the farmers' wives. Sometimes, she had resorted to just sending the invitation to "Mrs." She had sent nine invitations. Naturally, there was no way for them to reply, except for the few that went to the same Methodist church in Pavillion that she did. She guessed some must go to that Lutheran church at Kinnear. So, who knew how many would really come.

She didn't think the menfolk really understood that this kind of gathering would make the women better helpmates in the long run for their husbands. Women did need other women!

Jack wouldn't be in for the noon meal today. When he helped at the Elwoods', Charlotte would provide the meal. The same was true of when John was helping Jack; then, it was Sophia's turn to prepare the meal. John sure had raved about her lamb chops the last time he was here …

She put together a quick peanut butter and strawberry jelly sandwich for herself and Georgie and called the boy to lunch. Georgie took a quick run for the outhouse first. He burst into the house with all the enthusiasm of his four years. "Mommy! The spider in the outhouse was eating a fly. She had it wrapped up in her web in the corner by the door."

"Wow. I think our lunch will taste better than hers." She knelt down and gave the round little boy a hug.

His sun-streaked hair smelled unpleasantly of dirt and sunshine. She gave him a boost onto his stack of books at the table.

"After lunch," she said, pulling up her chair as she seated herself, "I'd like you to take a little nap. And when you wake up, I'll have a surprise for you." To announce at this point the visit of Kevin during their Club meeting would make it impossible for him to rest. The idea of a "surprise" would help him close his eyes fast so the surprise would happen faster. This would help her get the final touches on the upcoming meeting and her own clothes changed as well. She would even wear her high heels!

Awake from his nap, Georgie had barely had time to put on his clean overhauls when the surprise became evident. Kevin and his mother arrived for something Mrs. Elwood was calling "Club" and then here came some other children he'd never met, with their mothers, too.

"Hello. I'm Darla James. I live in that house with the stones around the mailbox." "I am Sadie Samson. I live over there behind the three big boulders." "Thanks for asking me here. I am Judy Stephers. My house is the one that has a big porch being built on the front. And I haven't met any of my neighbors out here yet." Georgie was delighted! There were four new friends to play with Kevin and him. Baby Deirdre and that other baby boy with the large lady were still just too small to count.

Georgie followed his mother's suggestion of taking them to his room to show them his toys. The children's laughter blended in with the sounds of spinning tops against the wooden floor, and the squeaking toy pig being squeezed a little too frequently.

Sophia enjoyed herself immensely as the women seated themselves in her living room and commented on the lovely grandfather clock she had carefully brought with her from Oklahoma. She chuckled with the women as they all talked of the ways in which their homes were still unfinished. Only a few had functioning indoor bathrooms.

Charlotte surprised Sophia by laughingly admitting to the group that she and her husband had begun to refer to their home as the "chicken house." She explained that the Elwoods had just gotten a good start on the "big house" they had planned to build since the time they'd drawn their homestead plot. "Our little one-room cabin is nice and warm and cozy, but it grows smaller with each addition to our family." Charlotte smiled and repositioned shy-acting Deirdre on her lap. "So, when we finally get the 'big house' finished a year or more down the road, we will convert our present little house into a chicken house. That's why we just keep the inside of it covered in Celotex and nothing fancier!"

Judy Stephers grinned through the smattering of freckles covering her face. "Our interior is just Celotex, also; and it makes a wonderful huge bulletin board, doesn't it?"

Darla shared with the group, "Our house is pretty simple, too, but nothing like my grandmother's. She was in the hills of New Mexico. Grandpa had ideas of a 'modern' house with low utilities. He actually dug them a cave and made glass in the roof of the house. I guess we'd call it a sky-light, now. I recall being there to visit when Grandmother said she needed some more shelves. And she actually just began to dig a new shelf in the dirt wall!"

"Well, then! That just makes us all living in pretty hotsy-totsy style!" Sophia's laughter was contagious.

Charlotte updated the others. "We will soon have another woman out here to join us. She is Mrs. Zanders. Her husband Henry has been building that log cabin out north of here. He's fetching her as we speak. He asked John and me all about the doctors and hospitals out here, as he says she is expecting just about anytime now."

"I hope it's safe for them to travel. If his truck jostles like ours does, it could be a baby along the road." Sadie shifted her large bulk in the dotted-Swiss dress, and placed her baby son on the other knee.

"I guess Henry rode the train back to meet her and help her get the last things packed. Then, they'll be taking the Burlington & Northwestern out here. They've put their things on a railroad flatbed car, too. Maybe that will be less bumpy than in a truck." Sarah amended.

A couple of the women tittered. "Less bumpy, more jerky," Sadie commented.

Sophia smiled to herself as she washed the dishes after the group had dispersed. Yes, this first Club meeting must surely be counted a huge success. The dessert had been enjoyed by all. One little girl had asked for seconds before her mother scolded her back to Georgie's room. It had been that Mrs. Stephers who spoke up to have the Club meeting at her house next month. She had drawn a map for them so they all had directions already. Sophia had volunteered to pass on the invitation to Flora Zanders. Bless her heart! Sophia surely hoped Flora Zanders' trip was going well as she made her way from back East to this new home of hers.

As he left the Zanders' place and headed his car towards home, Jack slowed the vehicle to look at the progress of the "improvements" on the other homesteads. His wife thought he had an "obsession" about looking at all the fences and the crops along the way wherever they drove these days. He had to admit it was quite pleasant to see the changes happening in the dirt and sagebrush turned farmland. Ho! There was a prairie dog standing on its back legs, holding its little front paws in front of its chest. As Jack's car came alongside where the animal was standing in its burrow out in the field, it darted quickly inside the hole.

Jack drove his car into the driveway and turned off the key. He rolled up the windows of the 1947 Ford. The breeze from the windows had felt good on this hot July day. That Henry sure did have some fine-looking sweet corn in his garden over there. Zanders must have planted a different type than Sophia had. Jack would have to ask him what kind he was growing, so he and Sophia could do the same next year. Why, they had even collected some cow manure from John to rake into their soil before planting their garden, and the corn looked downright stunted compared to Henry's.

Jack left the keys in the ignition as he swung out of the car. Nobody worried about robbers out here. It was really refreshing living out in the country. He'd been raised on a farm, but Sophia and he had been living in town after he got out of the military. He had to hand it to Sophia. She hadn't wanted to be a farm woman, but she knew how to stand beside her man. He was a lucky man.

Oh, yes. This was the day she was going to have her Club meeting. He hoped someone had come. John had said that Charlotte was planning to be there. It would be pretty disappointing for Sophia if it was just those two women again. They had become good friends, but Sophia was eager to see who else she could meet. She was quite a social soul.

"Daddy!" Georgie carried his toy truck around the corner of the house. "I had lots of friends here today. They came for Mama's Club."

"Ah, my boy," Jack lifted the boy into a bear hug against the dust that covered his clothes and sweat-streaked face, "it'll be a happy night in the old house tonight!"

CHAPTER 15

"But, They Smell."

"**W**HAT ARE YOU talking about? You are getting a cow so I can milk it? When on earth would I get the chance to go to a barn and milk a cow?" Flora's cheeks were reaching that pink shade that meant trouble.

"Darling, one cow doesn't take so long to milk. Patricia could be in her crib in the house while you milk. That is what my mother used to do with me when it was time to do the milking," Henry protested, "except she could get three cows milked before I was bawling so loudly all the neighbors were about to check to see what was wrong."

"No wonder you think the way you do—all that neglect you had as a youngster." Flora snorted and tossed her black curls. She patted her stomach. It seemed it would never get flat again since being so stretched with carrying baby Patricia.

"Now come on, Flora, Dear." Henry was using his best twinkling smile as he bent and looked into her face. "You have learned to tend the garden much better than you thought you would. Why, you even let Mrs. Elwood show you how to can the tomatoes and to make some pickles from the cucumbers. A little old cow isn't so bad. All you do is pull on the handles … teats, we call them."

"Why couldn't you milk her?" Flora shot back at him.

"Well, can't you see that I'm gone from daylight to dark now? I have been trying to get in the fencing and get some brush cleared from the ground so we can put in some crops next spring. There won't be money to go around if we don't start getting an income here. The inheritance from my grandpa is just about gone. I spent plenty of it on the logs for this house. But, that freed up the barracks lumber for that cow barn I've just finished. I've made four stanchions in it, thinking I can maybe have a dairy herd here one day before it's all said and done. And, we got enough wood from the barracks for the shed, and still some to spare now."

Flora was glad he had moved a bit in his subject from Grandpa's inheritance. She knew he had loved his grandpa very much, and that he felt he was honoring him, his hero, by building a strong farm here.

"I know you work hard, Dear," her tone had gentled. "It's just that cows smell so, and I am afraid it will take the strawberry scent from my hair." She stuck her lower lip out petulantly.

Baby Patricia began to whimper in the bassinet. She wasn't yet awake when Flora reached and pulled her into her arms. Henry watched and wondered if Flora would spoil the child, not letting her cry any time at all. His mother had told him that babies are supposed to cry; that's what makes their lungs strong.

"Well, Honey," Henry began, as he came and bent over where his wife had seated herself at the kitchen table, and had lifted her shirt to nurse the baby. He ran his hand gently down their baby's soft back. "If your hair were ever to smell like a cow, it would also be smelling like strawberries, and money! They say the smell of cattle is the smell of money."

"Humph," Flora, wasn't impressed, but her mood had softened, nursing their daughter.

"What do you say? Why don't we get a Holstein cow and I'll milk it in the mornings and teach you how to milk it in the afternoons? It will be nice to have our own milk instead of having to buy it from the Elwoods. And that way, we can enjoy some good thick cream, too. You could whip it and make some of those luscious cream puffs you made for us in Pennsylvania."

"How do we keep the cow giving milk? Doesn't she have to have a calf sometimes to keep the milk coming?" Jack could see from her question that she was considering the idea.

"Well, we take old Bossie to the neighbors who have a bull. We either pay the neighbor for Bossie's fun stay there, or we give them the calf as the payment. I think I'd rather keep the calf and let our herd grow …"

"Ah, is your tummy hurting?" The child had not stopped suckling, but her legs were drawing up to her abdomen and her little brows were pulling down. Flora supported the baby's back as she pulled the bundle from beneath her blouse and placed Patricia over her shoulder. She began to pat the baby's back with a firm rhythm.

Jack wondered how that whacking kept from injuring the child's spine. He might talk bravely of how it would be fine to leave the child in a crib during a milking, but he was not really even brave enough to hold the little girl by himself yet. A guy might do something wrong and let her head dangle or something.

The burp broke the silence. A bit more patting and it was time for nursing on the other side. "Okay, Jack, you go get your cow. I guess you'll have to get the small truck you've been talking about first. It would be too much to expect a neighbor to drive over and fetch the cow to meet with his bull."

"Ah, Flora, you know how much I've been hoping to get that truck. There's a used auto lot in Riverton I think we should visit Saturday."

"I'll get the grocery list ready. We spent twenty-nine dollars on groceries last month. I'll see if I can pare it down some this month." It had taken extra to stock up on some of the staples, like flour and sugar and laundry detergent, that she wouldn't need every month.

Actually, Flora was quite amazed at how well she had settled in here in just a couple of months. It had been so nice to be met with the blooming dianthus that Sophia Brown had transplanted along the garden border, telling

Jack that as long as he was watering other plants, he could water another row so there'd be pretty flowers for Flora.

Flora had felt well enough to put up curtains and get out the tablecloths, too, before the baby was born in August. She had enjoyed seeing her mother's crocheted wall hangings positioned against the sea green walls. She had loved putting out the velour green towels with the wonderfully crafted flowers in that fine bathroom that Jack had designed. She heard she was one of the few ladies in this Third Division Project to be able to relax in her own bathtub of hot water at the end of a tiring day. Jack was so goofy! He'd suggested it might even be big enough for the two of them.

Having burped the baby again, Flora rose and helped Jack to clear the lunch dishes from the table with her free hand. It was nice to have him come in and join her for dinner most of these days. Sometimes, when he knew the day ahead would be especially grueling, he'd have her pack him a cheese sandwich made on her baking powder biscuits. He was content with her putting some red Kool-Aid in his thermos on those days, too.

Jack gave her and Patricia a quick hug as he headed towards the door. He turned and gave her a wink before he closed the door behind him.

Kool-Aid. She wished he was as content to have Kool-Aid at night these days. When she'd first joined him here in Wyoming, Jack had seemed content to just spend time with her. They would share their dreams of the future way into the night, often imagining what it would be like to be real parents.

But, a couple weeks ago, when he'd run across that snake on the path to the house, he had changed his evening routine. From then on, it seemed he had to have a beer when he first sat down after getting washed up from the fields. Sure, it was just one beer, like he pointed out. And she was glad he wasn't insisting on visiting the bar in Pavillion he'd sometimes gone to when she wasn't yet out here.

Flora was trying not to make so much of his drinking the beer, although she really had no use for alcohol. She'd been taught that some people get into the stuff and just can't get out. Besides, it sure did stink. And she could swear it made his feet smell bad, too. However, it wouldn't do for a woman to boss her man around so much that he used her for an excuse to drink more!

CHAPTER 16

Faltering Harvest

"I KNOW." JACK shook his head and waved a bee away from his face. "I guess I over-watered that flattest stretch of mine. It looks like the water table has come up so much that I won't be able to get a combine in there until the ground freezes."

The mid-morning sun wasn't warming up the cool September day much. John sniffed the air. You could feel the autumn coming; the leaves would be dropping from his baby trees soon.

"Jack, we just don't know what this land will act like with the irrigating we have to give it. But, nothing could live in this desert except for the old sagebrush and cactus if we didn't give it a good watering. Maybe we'll learn better how to give it just the right amount of water.

Or maybe the land will stop pitching such a fit about getting a regular drink of it …" John was trying to soothe Jack, knowing he must feel pretty disappointed about the sogginess of his one oat field.

"But, it looks like you'll be able to get most of the harvest out, doesn't it?" John beckoned over the larger field.

"Yes. I am going to start on it tomorrow. You can use my combine when I'm done, if you want. When do you see yourself getting that alfalfa seed out?"

"Well, you know we got a good second cutting on that small patch I planned for hay. The haystacks ought to take my cows through the winter. But everything I study says I need to let the alfalfa seed ripen standing so it can be combined standing. It is looking like it won't be until the first of October or so." Now it was John slapping at the bothersome honeybee. Those beehives over on the Gaston place had made quite a contribution in pollinating his alfalfa field, but he wouldn't want to be stung.

"Glad you have a combine, Jack. It sure works better to be pulling one of those behind the tractor than those outdated threshing machines I see on the way to Riverton."

"John, I thought I heard you shooting your gun over at your place this morning. Did you get a rabbit for lunch?" Jack didn't handle compliments so well. It was easier to change the subject.

"No, I wouldn't eat a rabbit. I think they'll prove it is the fleas on the rabbits that have been carrying the polio. Darned shame about that little Sheriton boy dying of it."

Jack's face tightened. All the farmers were afraid of the dread disease. And it wasn't always just the children one heard of suffering from it. He knew of a young, strong adult in an iron lung now from polio. It was still unclear if he would even make it.

He went back to the subject of the gun. "So what were you shooting?

"It was a bobcat. But he jumped just as I fired and I missed." John chuckled, "Maybe that's why I wasn't so quick to talk about it!"

"Maybe it's the same one I've seen slinking around my place. I don't know how far they roam." Jack recalled a worse pest. "I was surprised to see a rattler out again yesterday, sunning himself on a rock. I thought maybe it was getting cool enough that we'd stop seeing them. Guess they'll be hugging the rocks more now."

"How many have you gotten this summer, so far?" John was adding up his snake conquests in his head.

"Last one I killed, last week, made it thirty this year." Jack's expression suggested that his friend couldn't possibly top that number.

"Gosh. How many of the rattlers are there out here? I got twenty-eight myself!" John exclaimed. "And that doesn't count the three or so that got away. Mostly, I cut off their heads with the shovel. But Charlotte and I also skid on them with the truck when we see them in the road. Twenty-eight! And your thirty! Together, we've killed fifty-eight rattlers! Jeez! It seems this country is just infested with them. But, no one out here has been snake-bit that I've heard of."

"No, I haven't heard of it, either. Looks like all those prayers are working."

"Well, I'm going to be praying that we can get in all the crops before the snow ruins them." John tipped his hat at his neighbor, and headed back toward his truck.

As he stepped inside and slammed the door, he glanced down at the boots that had saved him so many times from snakes this summer. Others out here might walk about in their tall cowboy boots, but he was grateful for these tall rubber hip-boots he used for irrigating. The snakes would strike them, but couldn't bite through them.

As he turned the key and the motor began to growl, he stepped on the clutch and shifted into low. Charlotte was actually getting pretty good at skidding on those snakes. She'd been the driver Saturday as they were heading to Riverton when they saw a snake slithering across the dirt road ahead of them.

"Hold on!" She'd automatically slung her right arm out across where Kevin was holding little Deirdre on his lap. Since he could see the snake ahead of them, too, John had been able to grab onto the dash to brace himself.

She'd backed up quickly and opened her truck door to look down to see if she had flattened the snake. When she'd shut the door, saying, "Nope, he's got that head going yet," Kevin had started to cry.

"Mommy, mommy," Kevin had pled, "he's going to put his head in here and bite us!"

John had put his arm around the child then and put Deirdre on his own lap. "Don't you worry, Son, we'll keep you safe from that old snake." The truck had jerked backwards again, nearly dying as Charlotte worked to get it into the right gear.

The truck had roared forwards then, before Charlotte stepped on the clutch, followed with the brakes, and put it into a skid again. Again, she backed up and swung her door open to look down to see if she'd accomplished death yet. This time, the snake wasn't going anywhere.

Charlotte had looked across at John with victory on her reddened face. "You don't need to climb down and get his rattles." She'd sounded terse with relief. "They aren't exactly intact anymore."

"I must be very, very careful around snakes," Kevin had murmured to himself as they again set out for Riverton.

John thought it was too bad little boys should have to worry so, and figured he really should talk to Charlotte again about letting the child go to the outhouse by himself. Maybe she was babying him a bit too much.

Soon, now cruising in fourth gear, his mind was back onto the combining. He would have to watch the moisture very carefully now as the crop matured. He didn't want to have it spoil with harvest time being so close.

CHAPTER 17

High Water Table

"I'LL BE BACK, Flora," Henry called. Flora was heading down the path to the milk barn, pail in hand. "I'm going to take my tractor over and try to help Jack Brown pull his tractor from his wet ground. John Elwood is there with his tractor, too."

Flora nodded and waved, shouting back for him to be careful.

Henry's step was quick as he went to the shed and dragged down a long chain to attach to his tractor. His tractor was one of the bigger ones on the Project and would be very helpful.

Henry was glad that John had waved him down as he had driven his pickup truck past them on the way back from "delivering that letter to the mail" at the Pavillion post office. It had been important for the letter to get out to Flora's father, but his beer had run out, too, and he was going to be a lot more comfortable knowing he had a supply. He'd left it in the back of the truck, covered with some canvas. No point in waving the beer in front of Flora. She didn't seem to look so happy whenever he tipped one back these days.

His John Deere was going its fastest, its putt-putt sounding strong and proud, as he steered it down the road towards Brown's place. He pulled down the flaps on his cap and snapped them, pulling up the collar on his coat against the October cold.

He didn't get much interaction with any of the men around here, now that he was no longer going to the bars. Not that he'd met many of the hard-working farmers in the bars, but a guy does need some fellowship with others.

He drove towards where he could now see John's Ford tractor already parked strategically near Jack's Allis Chambers.

John Elwood approached him. "Thanks for coming," he said, his voice loud over the John Deere. "It's pretty wet. Water table's come up on this piece of his. If you and I stay about this far back, I think we'll be out of the worst of it. How about you put your tractor right over there? Let me have your chain and I'll attach it to Jack's."

As he secured the chain around the hitch of the tractor, John looked at where Jack was tediously moving his legs, scraping the heavy mud from his boots onto the side of the huge tires of the tractor. There were already piles of mud thrown out from the rear tires' spinning. John and Jack had already used their shovels to try to get some of the worst of it from behind the tractor tires. "When I wave my hat, Jack, you put it into reverse and gun it."

Jack's unhappy face was becoming a bit more hopeful. "Okay. Two ought to do it."

John pulled the chain length out across the wet ground to Henry's tractor. "Pull up about three foot!"

As he attached the chain to the back hitch of Henry's tractor, he explained how, after mounting his own tractor, they must edge forward until the chains were taut and then stop. He told Henry to keep his eye on his hat, that he would wave it at Jack when it was time for all three to put their tractors in gear and pull.

When the chains were secure, the two tractors crept forward, side by side, until the chain was taut.

Then, John's Western hat was off, waving in the air, and the three tractors roared into a loud putt-putt growl together. It seemed John's and Henry's were going to just stay in place and wear off the tread from the tires, but then suddenly they began to lurch forward.

Looking over his shoulder, John could see that the Allis Chambers tractor was coming out of the field, mud flying to the sides. It looked like a good portion was landing upon Jack, the way he was ducking down. Henry kept his eyes on John, taking his cues from him.

The men didn't take any chances. They kept going with those tractors until they were in an area that no one could call soggy.

Jack beckoned for them all to stop, and he drove forward another few feet after the other two men had stopped so there'd be enough slack in the chains to detach them. When he had put his tractor into neutral, John and Henry got down from their tractors and removed their chains.

Jack turned off the ignition of his Allis Chambers and came to where the two neighbors were gathering their chains to toss behind their metal tractor seats. This task done, the three stepped aside from the loudest of the putt-putt sounds.

"I shouldn't have tried." Jack shook his head apologetically. "I was just so determined to get out all the oats I could on this first year, and get an accurate count of the yield. I thought I would check it out with the tractor first. Well, I guess I sure did!"

"Oh, I might have done the same thing." John wouldn't hold his friend's decision against him. "Guess you really do have to wait until it freezes to see what you can do with the field now."

"Yes. I am glad I didn't foolishly drag the combine into there, too. We might have torn it clear up trying to get that piece of equipment out!" Jack shook his head and thrust his hand out to shake Zanders' hand, and then Elwood's. "I sure do thank you both."

The warmth Henry felt inside almost heated up his outside! "It was my pleasure to help. Who knows? I may need the help myself one day. And, at that, you've already been up on my roof, saving my house from the storms last winter!"

John laughed, "Well, it looks like it'll be a bath in the old tin tub for me tonight. This is one muddy mess we've made out here."

The others' laughter joined his. "Damn! Look at that pile of mud I'll have to deal with when I do get into that frozen field." Jack shook his head. It appeared that this flat area of his field had two problems. It was the lowest area and soaked up too much of the run-off water, but also that looked like brown clay out there in the mud heap. Most of their land was sandy loam or even a gravelly mixture, so the clay was a bit of a surprise.

"Henry, how is your wife settling into your place over there?" John turned his attention to Zanders.

"Pretty well, actually," said Henry, his eyes practically sparkling with pride. "As we stand here, she is milking the cow!" His face was stretched in a wide grin.

"Great!" John was glad for the Zanders family, but he and Charlotte would sorely miss that nickel that Henry's family had paid them each week for the gallon of milk. Lately, they had resorted to raiding the piggy bank Kevin had brought to this country with them. That piggy bank held coins that Grandpa and the uncles had dropped in whenever they came to visit Kevin, all the way back to the time when he'd been a baby. Charlotte and he had hoped the money could one day contribute towards a college education for this smart little whip of theirs.

"Well, it'll be dark soon, and I've got my own cows to milk." John waved to the others and climbed up onto his tractor, turning the ignition. He made his way back to the dirt road, careful to stay away from the wettest places as he exited the field.

"Me, too. Must go." Henry made sure the chain had its hook secured in a link, there behind the tractor seat before starting his motor. He waved again to Jack, who was already turning to get onto his own tractor.

During the jarring ride back home, Henry reflected on the experience he'd just had. He could tell that Jack and John seemed to have formed a special friendship. It was right neighborly of John to ask about his wife. It had certainly been a good feeling when they'd won back the tractor from the mud!

He slowed down a bit as he turned the steering wheel into his own driveway. He drove his tractor to the area where he kept it, near the few pieces of equipment he now had gathered together.

As he walked towards the barn, he could see that Bessie was back in the shed, so he knew Flora had finished the milking.

"Hi, Honey!" He flung open the door and saw Flora setting the table, making sure the forks were on the left of the plates, the knives and spoons on the right. She had the freshly ironed, red-checkered napkins on the table tonight. What a pretty wife he had, standing there in her blue ruffled apron, with her dark hair and pink cheeks!

"Henry." Flora looked up, and came to him to give him a kiss on his cheek, wiping the dirt from one side of his face first, then rubbing her hand on her apron. "Were you able to help?"

"Yes, we worked together and did get that tractor pulled out. It was really stuck. Some of Henry's ground seems to be wetter than the rest. It's pretty tricky getting the crops out at the right time, before the frost comes and ruins things, but after the water table has receded. He won't get much good out of that part of his crop now, as he can't get into the field again until the ground is frozen solid."

"I hope ours goes better than that next year," Flora said. She was finally beginning to show a bit of interest in his progress with the field preparations.

The baby's cry rose from the bassinet, starting in little sleepy whimpers and gaining steam, finally rising into an angry wail.

Flora gave her husband another pat on the shoulder, and turned to her most pressing priority. Bending over the bassinet, she gathered up her daughter in her pink blanket. "Patty, Patty, it's okay. Mommy's here." Her face looked like an angel's, smiling down into the tinier one that was still emitting some sniffing sounds.

Henry hung his coat and cap upon the hook behind the door. He pulled out a kitchen chair and sat on it to pull off his muddy boots. He walked in his stocking feet to the kitchen sink and opened the cabinet underneath. He pulled a rag from off the pipe loop and wet it under the faucet. He headed back to wipe up the mud he had tracked in, onto the gray linoleum. He'd found that these acts of respecting her house helped Flora to be readier to help him with the outdoors work.

He raised the lid on the pot cooking on the stove for a peek before heading to the bathroom to wash up. Yum! His favorite, beef stew. He turned and grinned at Flora over his shoulder, and she smiled back at him from where she was seated on the rocking chair, humming as she nursed their little Patty.

Henry remembered the beer in the back of the truck. He hadn't gotten it to the icebox yet. True, the weather was cold enough that beer could be pretty tasty right out of the truck bed! But he felt content tonight, and didn't need anything to relax. He could skip it tonight.

CHAPTER 18

What Now?

"SO, JACK, WHAT happened to make that piece of ground so soggy that the tractor was stuck?" Sophia pulled the pans from the back of the stove where she had kept supper warming.

Jack's frustration was apparent on his sun-tanned face, and weariness was reflected in every tug as he pulled off his muddy outer clothing.

"I guess the ground was a bit lower there than it appears. The irrigation water must have run off some of the other ground and settled in there. It also has more clay than some of the other land. I'll have to find a way next year to irrigate there less often than the rest of it." Jack tried to be simple in his wording to Sophia. She was doing well to show so much interest.

Sophia left her post at the kitchen range and moved to stoop down and help Jack pull off his boots. She looked up into those glittery eyes, that always made her feel like the luckiest wife in the world. "Honey, that's too bad. The oats were looking so very good there, too."

"Yes. Probably because they got so much water! That's part of my dilemma. If I don't give the crop enough water, it will burn up. If it gets too much, I can't get in to harvest it. But," he forced a smile, "I ought to be able to make a bit of good out of it, even if I can't sell that bit. Most of the rest came out really well. It's good we got those granaries up last spring. One wouldn't have held the harvest!"

"Well, go wash, Sweetheart, and we'll have supper." She turned and called towards the bedroom where Georgie had been playing. "Georgie! Daddy's home! Time for supper!"

Sophia stepped out into the lean-to entry room and picked up the big metal kettle. After running water from the sink into it, she carefully carried it to the range, and struck a match to light the biggest burner under it. It wasn't Saturday, but Jack would be needing an extra bath this week! She filled and placed another of her pans onto the other back burner and lit that one, too. Jack was about finished with dipping his hands into the washbasin and splashing the water over his face again and again. He ran his wet hands over his unruly brown hair and patted it flat. He pulled the towel from the oven door and roughly rubbed his face.

"Mmmmm," Jack said appreciatively, looking more like his old self as he turned and grinned at his wife. "Something is smelling really, really good."

"Daddy!" Georgie streaked around the corner and grabbed Jack around his long-john leg, and tugged at the buttoned drop seat on the long underwear.

Jack leaned down and swung the boy up for a hug. "Watch that yanking at my back door, Son," he laughed.

He kissed Georgie's head as he set him down on the stack of Sears and Roebucks catalogues atop his chair.

"Your daddy was in a big tractor parade today." He smiled wryly over the child's head at Sophia, and pulled out a chair to seat himself in front of the plate of hash beef. Sophia had placed a small dessert dish of home-canned peaches at the top of each individual's plate.

"Georgie, no!" Sophia tapped on the hand of the small boy who was sneaking a spoonful of peach juice. "That's your dessert. No peaches until you eat your supper … Oops, the salt and pepper." She dashed back to the cupboard again.

Seated at last, Sophia asked if Georgie wanted to say the prayer.

"No, Daddy can do it," said Georgie, beaming at his father.

"Lord, we thank you for this food, for the hands that prepared it, for a loving family, and we trust you with the price of our harvest. Amen."

"I guess you'll soon be driving it to the Farmer's Co-op to sell it," Sophia ventured.

"Yes, maybe you'll want to go with me. We can leave Georgie to play that day with Kevin and Deirdre." He helped the little child retrieve some hash beef he'd chased off his plate onto the tablecloth. "Although I must say, you sure are a good boy about playing all alone."

Sophia regarded her husband with her blue eyes and tossed her long blond curls. The rags she wound in those curls once a week sure did work magic. He peered more closely at her mischievous expression. "What?" he asked.

"Even if it is good he can play alone, it's beginning to look like that won't be a forever situation." Sophia's smile would hardly fit on her face.

"You mean …? Oh, my gosh. With so few tries?" His tone was incredulous.

"Shhh …" Her face pinkened and her head jerked briefly towards the boy. "I'm almost positive."

"Daddy, after supper, do you want to help me make a parade with my toy tractor and my cars and trucks?"

"Yes, my son, I do at that!" Jack was feeling newly energized. "But first, I need to give your momma a big hug." He rose from the table and squatted down in front of his wife and gave her a long hug, and finished with a peck on the mouth.

"She made us a good supper, didn't she?" Georgie was proud he knew the reason for the sudden show of affection. When the adults responded with a burst of laughter, he happily joined in.

A loud banging at the door broke the atmosphere. Jack quickly got to his feet and pulled on his pants. Little Georgie jumped down from his tall perch to stand behind his daddy and peek around him to see who might be outside the door.

"Hello, Henry. Sorry to bother you again. But I've got my family in the car. When I got home tonight, I found that Deirdre was burning up. She won't stop crying. We can't seem to get the fever down. We've got to get her to the hospital. We're thinking it could be that polio."

Jack hoped the dread didn't show on his face, the way it felt inside. "No. No. It's probably just a bad case of the croup, John. How can I help? You want to leave Kevin here with us for the night?"

By now, Sophia was at the door, too. "Yes, you must leave him here. He can sleep the night with Georgie. And if you need him to stay more days, it'll be okay. Let's see, will you need your two cows milked, too?"

"I hate asking you to do that worse than anything," John kicked his foot and looked down. "But if you are willing to do it, that would be a big worry off my mind. I will tell you what: I'll have to pass back by your place on the way home from Riverton. So, if I don't come by and tell you I'm home by milking time, I'd sure appreciate your going over to do it."

"What time have you been doing your milkings?" Jack wondered if he still knew how to squeeze those teats to really accomplish a stream of milk. He'd not milked cows since he was a teenager and had sworn off any such thing.

"Well, I do the morning milking at six, but if you get there by seven the cows could live with it. I give them each some oats and tie each one to that post in the corner of the shed as I milk her. What am I telling you this for? You've seen me do it. Rope's hanging on the shed wall, as is the milking stool. I take a clean washrag to wash each cow's teats and udder. I just strip each one of the teats first to knock out the manure before I start keeping the stream in the bucket. The clean milk buckets are behind the door there in the house. And Charlotte's got several milk bottles washed on the counter. You better bring it home and drink it if this runs into the night milking, too. Actually, why don't you bring at least one bottle home even from the morning milking. We pull up that rope at the well pit and bring up the big basket we lower down to keep the milk good. Keeps things pretty nice. Never warms, but protects from the freeze as well, way down there so deep."

Jack could see that John was having trouble concentrating on details and was restless to get onto the road. Riverton was forty miles away, and the hospital surely another eight. It would be a long, worried ride with a sick baby.

Jack was already sliding into the coat that Sophia had brought from its hook on the wall. "Let me bring the boy in. You can just get back into the truck and head on out." The air was bitterly cold as Jack pulled the house door behind him and matched his steps to the swift ones of his friend's.

As John climbed back up into the driver's side, pushed off the emergency brake, and worked the clutch to shift the truck into neutral, Jack was helping Kevin climb around Charlotte who sat at the other truck door, holding the blanket over her daughter's head to protect it from the air that already screamed of winter. A steady whimper came from underneath the blanket. John's heart dropped. One knew the sound of a very ill child. It was so different from that of a petulant or frustrated one.

"Come on, Kevin." Jack's strong arms wound around the child. "You'll play here with Georgie while Mom and Dad go to town."

Kevin was snapping the earflap strap under his chin. He turned to wave at his mother and father and the blanket that held his baby sister as Mr. Brown slammed the truck door shut for his momma.

Jack held the boy against his shoulder, shielding him from the wind as John reversed the truck and turned towards Riverton. He couldn't see into the truck cab, but he knew his friend would be touching his finger to his forehead in his characteristic half wave, half salute.

Sophia was opening the door as Jack arrived on the step with his armload. She started to reach for the child, but Jack gave her a knowing frown and turned and set the child down onto his feet without her help. He had not forgotten her good news.

"Di Dee is sick!" Kevin's naive tone shared news, but held no worry.

"Yes." Sophia's voice was soft. "But the doctors will fix her up. And you are here to keep Georgie company. But do you need some supper first?"

"No. Mommy let me make my own peanut butter and jelly sandwich. I even cleaned up all the jelly I spilled on the floor."

"Whewie. That sounds like a very big boy," Sophia said, holding back her laughter and wondering how long Charlotte's feet would be sticking to her wooden floor.

The little boys' feet clattered down the hall towards the toys. "I'll let you sleep with my teddy bear," offered Georgie, his voice fading into his bedroom.

John was pulling off his coat again. The boiling water was rattling their pans on the burner and sending steam into the air. Now it would be a bit trickier taking a bath tonight. John seated himself and finished his supper. Charlotte busied herself picking up the remains from Georgie's place, as he would be too excited to eat more now. She sat down and finished her dish of canned peaches.

"So. It's a hard country here sometimes, Hon." John felt a lump in his throat. "We must keep this new one of ours and that little girl of the Elwood's in our prayers tonight."

Charlotte rose and put her arm around her husband's tired shoulder. "God will look after us all, Jack. He always does. I'm going to finish up clearing the table here so that you can start your bath. I'll get your clean things and a towel."

She returned with the towel, a washrag, and his clean long-johns. "You know where the tub is, there in the service porch. I'm going to go put the boys on the chamber pot and help them pick up their toys. I'll get them settled for bed by reading them a book while you take your bath."

"You'll need to take awhile settling them in. I've got to make a trip to the outhouse first." John took another long drink from his glass and set it down in the metal dishpan with the other dishes. He would refill one of the kettles with water to boil when he had filled his bath. Sophia would need warm water for the dishes yet.

His coat collar once again pulled up high over his ears, Jack strode from the house and headed in the dark down the familiar path to the outhouse. The moon was up and the stars were out tonight. He could hear the forlorn cry of the coyotes across the canal. Good thing they stayed over there. The Elwoods didn't need a hungry coyote sniffing around their cows in addition to everything else going on right now.

CHAPTER 19

The Dread Polio

"WE'LL HAVE TO keep her here for a few days." Doctor Clarion's face was serious. "We took some samples, but we won't know for a few days just what the trouble is. We may need to do some intravenous things to get her fever down. When it is 104, we worry."

"Poor baby," said Charlotte, who obviously would have much rather had any needles inserted into her own arm. "Can I stay in the chair there by her crib?"

"No. It's too hard on the babies when they sense their mothers are worrying. We have some fine nurses here. They'll watch over her. You would do better to go home and get a good night's sleep once we get her settled into the crib in her room."

"But, I think Charlotte can keep our youngster calmer." John was uneasy with this turn of events, too. "Besides, we live forty miles away, out by Pavillion. We have no phone. We absolutely have no way for you to call us if anything turns worse." He looked towards Charlotte and could see the tears swimming in her eyes.

"Hmmm …" The doctor went to the door of his office and retrieved the crying baby from the nurse who had just arrived back. The child's cries were erupting in hiccups. Doctor Clarion ran his hand over the baby's forehead and peered with concern into her unhappy face. He unbuttoned her little sweater and let the cool air hit her feverish body. He glanced at Charlotte, and seeing her already on her feet, handed Deirdre to her.

"Let's do this. I'll let you settle her into the crib. You can stay until they get the intravenous fluids started on her. It may upset you, because we'll have to tie her arms down so she won't pull it out. Perhaps you could help her know it's okay. Then, we'll show you to the lobby. There are some chairs out there. Probably not too comfortable, but no one will mind if you rest out there. We can call you if there's any serious change." The doctor shook his head. "It will be a long night for the two of you."

"Thank you, Doctor," the Elwoods' grateful voices sounded in near unison.

The doctor pulled the black phone from where it nestled on the wall and spoke with authority. "We have one here that needs to get into a pediatric bed right away. She'll need a crib. We want her where we can watch her closely … No. We don't know yet. May be good to put her in a room where she's by herself until the test results come back. We've swabbed her throat and got some urine and some blood tests. Send someone down here right away to get her. I've permitted her parents to stay with her until she is settled in a bit. Then you can show them to the lobby for the night. They live some forty miles out in the country and have no phone and are pretty worried."

It was another hour before little Deirdre had cried herself to sleep. Her hair fell in damp curls from the perspiration created by the non-stop crying. John put his arm around Charlotte's shoulder as she stood up from bending for one last kiss on the wet and flushed, tear-streaked little face. Even though he wasn't given to public demonstration, he didn't take his arm from around her shoulder as they left Deirdre's room, following the beckoning nurse.

Charlotte kept her eyes on their guide, who was showing them towards the lobby. The heavy-set nurse waddled in front of them with more speed than one would expect, her stiff, white cap making her body look like an upside-down cone. Charlotte shook her head. What weird thoughts she had at times like this. It was as though the pictures hanging from the walls in the hallway took on more detail. Probably her mind's way of diverting her attention from the worry of leaving her child farther and farther behind. John's body was warm and comforting beside her. He must be very worried, too.

"There. We can get you each a pillow and a blanket. If you pull the chairs against the wall, you can probably prop the pillow behind your head." The nurse was pointing a round finger at very straight-backed wooden chairs. At least the chairs could be moved nearer the wall.

"Thanks, Nurse. We'll accept the pillows and blankets. Please do tell us if there is a change." John was unsuccessful at his attempt at a smile.

"And, Nurse." Charlotte was eager for the nurse to get back to her child, but there was so much to tell her. "Her name is Deirdre. She likes it when we sing "London Bridge Is Falling Down" if she's tired but can't get to sleep, and she will say 'dink' when she's thirsty, and she's big enough to drink from a cup now, and …"

"Charlotte, Hon," said John, as his hand rubbed her forearm with caution, "let the nurse get back to Deirdre. She will need her."

"But, promise you'll call me if you need me," Charlotte said, steadying her quivering lower lip. It wouldn't do to prove the doctor right–that upset parents would upset the little ones.

"I promise. Now I'll be right back with the blankets." The nurse's movement was almost fluid as she disappeared from sight.

"Oh, John." Charlotte turned into her husband's hug and laid her head upon his shoulder. "Well, let's move these chairs." She wiped away her tears with the back of her hand and engaged in couple of swift, determined sniffs.

He was glad to have something he could do to help. He hurried to lift the chairs to the side of the room. John knew being helpless was definitely not something he'd ever done with a lot of grace. It was good there weren't other people in the lobby just now. Who knew what kind of diseases people would have in a lobby like this. Diseases! John's heart beat faster with the recognition that it might be his own child with a dread disease. And who knew what kind of trouble that would mean for his unborn baby if his wife had been subjected to some terrible illness. Well. He sure wasn't going to mention this to Charlotte. Her face looked ten years older tonight as it was.

A young, lithe woman dressed in a green uniform arrived with pillows and blankets. "Nurse Thompson told me to bring these to you. She's a very good nurse, just loves the little ones, and will take very good care of your daughter," said the girl. She sounded like a mind reader to Charlotte. John thanked her, and the two attempted to settle into the chairs. Eventually, with his coat rolled behind her lower back, Charlotte was able to rest somewhat comfortably. John didn't really care if his bones ached. He didn't have a baby inside to protect.

The two were quiet, and each knew the other was praying. Charlotte was calling out so loudly to the Lord in her mind that she wouldn't be surprised if it sounded out loud. *Lord, please, please, please make little Deirdre be alright. Please help the doctors and nurses to be gentle with her. Don't let my baby girl be afraid and have no one to comfort her.* As her head tilted back against the pillow, tears were sliding quietly down her cheeks.

John was praying, too. *Heavenly Father, you have a parent's heart, too. You know how it is to love your child and want your child to be safe. I lift our little girl up to you, Heavenly Father. Please help her grow well. And protect the rest of us from dread diseases, too. Please don't let anything happen to that little baby deep inside my wife's belly now, either. Heavenly Father, I know I am not always perfect, that I disappoint you with my impatience. And sometimes I say the weather won't hold and I don't have time to quit farming and go to church. Please forgive me for that. Don't punish my child for my sins. I promise: help Deirdre and the rest of the family be well, and I'll go to church regularly!* John's calloused hand sneaked up to wipe a tear from each eye before his wife could see.

"G'night, Honey." Charlotte's voice sounded so tired. "God loves Deirdre even more than we do."

"I know, Char." John's voice sounded husky to her, even though he was almost as close to her, there braced against the wall, as when they lay in bed, side by side. "Get some rest. The baby will be okay. I just feel it."

John listened for the sound of her gentle snore. It didn't come right away. Before she slept, he could hear her humming quietly, "Smile and the world smiles with you, weep and you weep alone."

As her humming became more intermittent, John shifted his weight and chose to think of things outside the hospital. Funny how a fellow could come to love a woman and the children she bore. He'd always considered himself a practical man and it made more practical sense to love the land. And he was feeling some fierce protectiveness towards this Wyoming land that was now his, at that! It was a good thing, maybe a

God-given thing, to have neighbors like the Browns. He wouldn't have to give a second thought to Kevin while he was with them. They would be treating him like their own son.

The cows would give Jack a bit more headache. Jack didn't seem to want to mess with cows. John guessed nothing too bad could happen with Jack looking after them, other than Jack maybe getting kicked off the stool if he forgot to sit right, or (and John smiled at the thought), he might even get peed on if he didn't recall what a cow's rising tail meant! But he imagined Jack would be sure to empty the cows' udders fully so they didn't get mastitis. That could ruin the milk until he had given the cows enough medication, injected into each teat.

John's thoughts were starting to wander now, and he reeled them back to dwell on the thought that he was really a very fortunate man. He had a loving and downright pretty wife, two sweet children and one in the oven. And, a chance to raise his children on his own land. He was enjoying cutting a farm from dirt and sagebrush, cactus and greasewood. He even felt that the land was more his own every time he killed a rattler. Too bad he'd not gotten the bobcat yet.

He was praying another request to his Heavenly Father to heal little Deirdre when he fell asleep and his louder snores rose over Charlotte's softer ones.

"Mr. Elwood. Mrs. Elwood." The round nurse was leaning over the couple tilted against the wall.

Charlotte's eyes snapped open. "What? What? Is something wrong?"

The nurse's smiling eyes met the young mother's startled ones. "No. It's morning. Your baby is awake. She might be coaxed to eat some breakfast if you can join her."

John had risen from his chair and was trying to stretch the cramps from his back. His head ached and a cup of coffee sure would taste good. "How is Deirdre?"

"We were able to get her fever lowered. She is still quite sick, and unhappy to be strapped down. We know she'll be glad to see her momma. Mr. Elwood, why don't you take that hall down to the hospital cafeteria and get yourself a bite of breakfast, so Mrs. Elwood can take a turn down there after a bit?"

"Alright." John would have liked to peer in at Deirdre first, but he didn't want to press; he remembered that it was out of the ordinary to be able to stay at all.

"I brought a bit of money." Charlotte pressed a silver dollar into his palm. John decided to trust her that this dollar could be split for their breakfast. He would not worry just now about whether they would need more later today.

Charlotte quickly piled up their blankets and pillows on one chair and headed down the hall alongside the nurse, who was again moving like a duck.

"I'm not sure I introduced myself last night. I am Nurse Thompson. My shift is ending now, and it will be easier for the next nursing shift to adjust to you being here in the lobby if those nurses start by seeing you in the baby's room." She opened the door to the small room and they moved past an empty crib to the one where Deirdre lay.

The hiccupping cries tugged at Charlotte's heart and made her move faster, leaving Nurse Thompson a few steps behind.

Deirdre looked so small lying there with her arms stretched out to her sides, with her eyes closed and her lower lip drooping. Her miserable cries were moving her little chest up and down. The fingers of one hand had found the satin binding of her small blanket and she was rubbing it between her thumb and forefinger. Charlotte wished the hospital would have let the baby keep her favorite "blankie." It must be in a cupboard here somewhere, along with the baby's clothes. She could see the child was in a small, white hospital gown. Well, at least they had changed her sometime between when Charlotte had left her and now. As she bent over the tiny child, she could see that Deirdre's hair was in moist ringlets, probably from working herself up, crying so hard. It just wasn't fair that a little one like this had to go without her mama! Charlotte's belly twisted in guilt. What kind of a mother was she, to have been able to give in to sleep while her baby sobbed in another room, scared, sick and alone? Oh, no! Her belly was twisting with more than guilt. Charlotte took a step back before her child could realize she was there.

"I must use a bathroom. I'm going to vomit." Charlotte drove the words out urgently.

"Quickly. In here." Nurse Thompson guided her a few paces down the hall to a public bathroom. "I'll wait out here."

As Charlotte opened the bathroom door again and straightened her hair with a weak smile, Nurse Thompson looked at her sternly. "Do you have what the baby has?"

"No." Charlotte's smile was deeper now. "I have morning sickness. I'm pregnant with our next one."

"Oh, well. Good. I think, anyway … come on, let's see to this little girl of yours. She sounds very much awake now."

It was so good to touch her child and see that she at least didn't seem any worse than when they'd brought her to town. "Mommy is here, Sweetie. Don't you cry. These nice doctors and nurses are going to make you all better."

Deirdre wasn't looking convinced, wincing as Nurse Thompson approached her.

"It's the shots. They learn pretty soon who brings the shots," Nurse Thompson said, sounding a bit sad. She looked down into the little face that was readying to break into a wail. "Bye, little one. I'll see you again tonight."

She turned to Charlotte and said, "Good-bye, Dear. You make sure you eat something, you hear? And please do get some rest. It is very important that you keep healthy, so you can take care of both your children."

"Three. I have a son at home, too. He's five now. He's with the neighbors. They've been kind enough to watch him and milk our cows." Charlotte felt like she was blabbering, and this poor nurse was tired and needed to get home.

"Look, here's your breakfast, Baby." Nurse Thompson took the tray from the young man who had carried it into the room. "Now, Mrs. Elwood, see if she will drink some of the juice, and try to interest her in the scrambled eggs. If she won't take the eggs, maybe a bit of this apple juice. But, don't force her. She may be too ill to eat. Hopefully, she'll at least take the juice …" She waved to Charlotte and headed down the hall.

It was a relief to be alone with her baby. But, how could the poor little thing eat lying down like that? Somehow it had felt comforting to have the large nurse nearby.

A cheery-faced woman with a red birthmark down one cheek rustled into the room in her nurse's uniform. "So, who do we have here?" She smiled at Charlotte and leaned warmly towards Deirdre. The infant began to cry abruptly.

"Uh, oh! Somebody has had to have some shots, huh?" The woman moved to the end of the bed and pulled off the chart. "How do you say her name? Deirdre? I'm guessing you are Mom?"

"Yes. I'm Charlotte Elwood. The doctor was nice enough to let my husband and me stay in the lobby last night. We were very worried about Deirdre, and we live forty miles out in the country. We don't have a phone, and we couldn't be reached if something went wrong with her. Nurse Thompson was very kind, and let me come feed her breakfast."

"My name is Sarah. I'll be her nurse today. I'll be in here a lot. But here, let's roll the bed up a bit." Sarah was loosening the child's restraints a bit so that the bed rail wouldn't pull too tightly as the bed was raised. Sarah stooped at the end of the bed and turned the crank a couple times.

"Darling, here's some nice juice. It tastes yum, yum, yummy!" Charlotte attempted to put some excitement into her voice. Deirdre's shadowed eyes registered interest as her mother put the little cup to her lips. She took a small sip. Then, the child laid her head back tiredly.

"Mumma. Mumma." Deirdre tried to tug at her bound wrists.

Charlotte massaged one of the child's hands even as she raised the cup again. "I know, Darling. Your hand is there just for now. It won't always be stuck. But, let Mommy be your hands. Look, here's more of that good juice again. Yum, yum, yummy."

Almost listlessly, Deirdre made another obedient try. Her sip was only a bit longer this time. As she laid her head back, she turned her face dismissively from the juice.

John moved in the doorway, his brows drawn worriedly. With forced cheer in his voice, he said, "There's my girls! How's daddy's little Di Dee?"

Deirdre began to cry, her lower lip stuck out, peering through teary eyes at her father. Sarah crossed her arms and rocked back on her heels as she chuckled, "We can see who's got Daddy wrapped around her little finger."

"Nurse Sarah, this is my husband John. John, Sarah will be taking care of Deirdre this next shift."

John smiled quickly in the direction of the nurse, but kept his eyes on the sobbing child. He bent over her and kissed her damp forehead, stroking her ringlets. "It's going to be okay, Di Dee. This is a place that makes little girls feel better. And Jesus is here with you, too. Mommy and Daddy love you."

"Okay, Deirdre. Time for more juice." Charlotte's hand behind Deirdre's neck helped bring her reluctant head forward. The juice had trickled gently into the baby's mouth only a little before she pulled back weakly, saying "No. No."

A bell down the hall caught Nurse Sarah's attention. "Mr. and Mrs. Elwood, I will be back shortly. But, here's what I want. I want you, Mrs. Elwood, to go down to the cafeteria and catch a bite to eat. John, stay with your daughter until I get back. Just talk to her. See if she can be coaxed into a bite of those eggs. But don't put anything at all into her mouth if she doesn't want it. We do have intravenous nourishment going into her arm there. Your presence will be encouragement for her."

As the nurse left the room, Charlotte leaned over and kissed her baby's cheek, as she accepted the sixty cents John pressed into her hand. "Mommy loves you, Deirdre," Charlotte's voice soothed.

As she headed out the door, she could hear her child's whimpering, "Mumma, Mumma ..." Charlotte and John both knew she wouldn't be bothered with breakfast this morning if it weren't for the unborn child needing her care, too.

Charlotte had hardly passed out of sight down the corridor when Dr. Clarion entered the hospital room. John rose from where he was attempting to coax the pale little face on her pillow to turn towards the spoonful of scrambled egg.

"Well, young lady, looks like you have the troops here." The doctor sounded hearty as he picked up the chart hanging at the end of her bed. Deirdre did not look impressed to see him.

"It's like this," he said to John. "We don't yet know all about what might be wrong. Her chest sounds like it might have a trace of pneumonia. We don't think that was the original or main problem. We cannot rule out polio yet, but we're pretty hopeful at this point that she has missed that one."

John let out a deep sigh. He hadn't realized he was holding his breath.

The doctor continued, "The nurse tells me your wife is pregnant. We really must not have her in this hospital where there is so much polio. You realize that if she got even a slight case of polio, it could mutate the baby? You have no phone at all?"

"None." John shook his head and reached out and stroked Deirdre's curls, which she was shaking back and forth on the pillow with a soft moan.

"Well, how far to somewhere with a phone you might borrow? A neighbor's, perhaps?"

"No. No one out there has one." John shook his head. "We would've given a lot for a phone just now, though."

"Actually, I'm wondering, who could I call to tell you there is a problem if things get worse, or even if there is really good news and we decide to send your child back home?"

John stood quietly, his brow furrowed and one of his boots tapping on the floor. "I don't know, Dr. Clarion. We live forty miles from here. Why don't we do this? I'll take my wife home. She'll be able to watch over our five-year-old son, who's staying with the neighbors now. Then I will come back every day and check, or stay over a day or two if things seem worse. To be truthful, it is costly driving back and forth, as well, and you know I will be paying the hospital bill out of my pocket. We may be able to sell one of our two cows to get that paid a bit sooner."

Dr. Clarion looked at John with new respect. "Did you say you are out near Pavillion? You aren't one of those homesteaders out there, cutting your farm out of dirt and greasewood, are you?"

John mastered a tired smile and patted his daughter again. "That, and cactus and sagebrush, and a couple dozen rattlers, too."

"Okay. Let your wife say good-bye to the little one here and then you take Mrs. Elwood home. If you decide that you, without your wife, must camp out here in the lobby to have any peace of mind, we can tolerate that. You might want to pack a couple items for yourself in a bag so you can stay fresh while here. Your wife probably will need you to help me encourage her to wait at home. I don't imagine my asking her to leave will go over so well."

"I heard that," Charlotte said as she entered the room briskly. "So, what is it you are saying, Dr. Clarion?"

The doctor's eyes went to her abdomen. "I am considering your next baby, too. We can take care of your little Deirdre here. But we can't help the outcome of your unborn baby if it gets exposed to polio here."

Charlotte's eyes were wide. "What? Is that what she has? Is it polio?"

The doctor started over. "No. I mean, it is undetermined yet as to what all is wrong here. But she does seem to be stabilized with the treatment we are giving her. I am equally concerned about your fetus. A fetus can react badly to your exposure to polio anywhere within these hospital walls. I really need you to wait at home. Get plenty of fresh air out there on the farm and take care of yourself, and your, what did your husband say? Your five-year-old boy, too."

Charlotte had joined in the touching of the baby's ringlet curls. John put his arm about her. "Hon, I'm going to take you home to get you away from hospital germs. They may be able to let Deirdre go home in a couple days. I will take you home, get a good night's rest, milk the cows for the morning, and head back here for a couple days. If I she gets well enough to bring home by the end of that time, I'll do so. Otherwise, I'll come back and check with you, because I know you'll be worried."

Charlotte could hear the "I mean business" tone in John's voice. "Okay. Let me sing her a song first."

Charlotte's gentle sing-song of "London Bridge" soon had the restless child growing quieter and her little eyes closed. Nurse Sarah had stepped back into the room to watch this calming effect. She promised the worried mother that she could try to help in this way, too.

As John and Charlotte stepped quietly to the door, with the doctor following, they could see Nurse Sarah beginning to change the intravenous-drip bag hanging on the pole. Charlotte took one more look at her child before tearing her eyes away and striding ahead of John and the doctor towards the exit. John gave a knowing look to the doctor and silently mouthed the words "Thank you" as he hurried to catch up with his wife.

As they climbed into the Ford truck, both could feel the tiredness reaching into their bones. John backed the truck from its parking spot before he spoke.

"She'll be okay, Hon," John said, his voice husky. As he drove quietly into the brisk fall evening, he could see his wife turn her head and face the window with her hands against her cheeks. The shaking of her shoulders told him she was quietly sobbing, too weary to hold back the tears any longer.

CHAPTER 20

Harsh Realities

"OH. MY GOSH, Charlotte how did you ever stand it?" Flora lowered a brow with concern. "I don't even know how I'll stand it when little Patty grows up and gets married! I can't imagine leaving her in a hospital while she's still so little, like your dear Deirdre." Flora pushed a stray black curl from her forehead.

Charlotte placed her letters in the post office window, and laid her package addressed to her mother there, too. This year Mama's birthday was on Thanksgiving. She peered around for Mr. Clark and then pushed her finger down on the bell to summons him. She turned back to Flora. Her maternity smock was pushing out in front between the open buttons on her wool coat.

"Prayer, Flora. That's all we have sometimes, isn't it? That wonderful preacher from our Methodist church drove out to our house and prayed with me one day. And John was so wonderful. He went back and stayed at the hospital until she could come home those three days later. And I'll never be able to thank Jack and Sophia enough. They watched our boy Kevin, plus they milked the cows while we were gone. And when I came back, Jack kept looking in on the cows, making sure I had enough hay broken loose to feed them. So, Flora, how are you and Henry doing over there? I guess Henry must be watching Patricia for you while you're here, huh?"

"Actually, he's a bit under the weather right now, and since Patty was sleeping, I just thought he could be useful and tend to her while I'm gone. It's not like she'll need feeding." Flora tried to keep the disgust from her voice. Under the weather, indeed! He'd been so hung-over this morning he'd complained when she let the firewood fall to the floor. Not that he'd been going to get up and carry it in! He'd said he had a meeting to go to last night and she guessed she could tell where that meeting must have been held. After all, there was only one bar in this little spot in the road they called a town! And she'd be darned if she'd pick him up a case of beer like he asked for. What kind of lady would they think her to be?

Flora was aware Charlotte was looking intently at her, and quite a silence had ensued. "Well, I hope it's nothing serious with Henry. John sometimes gets throwbacks to the malaria he had in Japan during his time in the service. It passes in twenty-four hours or so, but he sure does bundle up warm and shiver with it. I guess our men went through quite a bit in the service, huh, Dear?"

"Perhaps. Oh, there's the postmaster." Flora was sorry she'd even mentioned Henry being "sick." It was all she could do to hold her tongue.

"Well, hello, ladies!" Mr. Clark was always friendly, and looked nice in his freshly ironed Western-cut shirt. "Looks like we need to send a package to Kansas. And what will you be needing, Mrs. Zanders?"

Flora spoke over the noise of him smacking the ink stamper down on the package. "I have a slip here saying that there's a package from my mother." She held the colored slip up as she waited her turn behind Charlotte. She sure hoped it would be that new dress Mom had been smocking for Patty. It was supposed to have tatting for a collar and at the edge of the puffed sleeves, too!

"Thanks, Mrs. Elwood," said Mr. Clark, taking Charlotte's quarters, nickels, and dime and counting them out. "That's exactly the right amount."

Charlotte stepped to the side of Flora and waited for her to finish her business. She watched her friend's eyes light up when Mr. Clark handed her a sizeable package wrapped in brown paper.

"Sorry he couldn't get it into the mailbox," said Mr. Clark.

"Well. Thanks so much. I'm really going to enjoy this." Flora's cheeks were pink as usual now, and she started out the door of the tiny building with Charlotte right behind her.

"Flora, we're going to have Club at my house again next Friday afternoon. We do hope you'll be able to join us. You remember, it's just fine to bring children."

"Thanks, Charlotte. Two o'clock, isn't it?" Flora saw Kevin sitting proudly in the Elwoods' truck cab on the passenger side, holding his sister Di Dee. The truck motor was gently running so as to keep the heater on. Flora hoped her daughter would one day be as obedient as that little boy of the Elwood's. A more unruly child might run the truck right through the post office.

"Yes. And Flora," Charlotte said, laying her hand on Flora's arm before opening the truck door, "don't forget that we neighbors help each other. And if you ever need a hand at all, you just holler."

"Sure. Yes. Of course." Flora pulled her coat collar tighter and hurried, with a wave to the little boy smiling inside that truck, towards her own vehicle. Maybe she'd been stupid to leave Henry in charge of Patty. She'd better be sure her anger didn't put her child in jeopardy just because it felt like a proper punishment for Henry's drunkenness.

CHAPTER 21

A Wyoming Blizzard

IT DIDN'T SEEM like the snow would ever quit. Jack had cut the footpath to the driveway six times already. He had used the blade on the tractor to push the driveway clear three times. It looked like they were in for a long winter. He had snorted when he heard the radio announcer say during breakfast this morning, "It's a beautiful day in Fremont County!" That darned announcer said that every day no matter what! "Yes, it's beautiful, with snow falling, measuring eighteen inches. It's twenty below zero in Lander."

A beautiful day in Fremont County! It was bitterly cold, that's what it was! His fingers were already nearly numb in his gloves as he pulled his sheepskin cap farther down on his forehead and pushed up the sheepskin coat collar.

Jack didn't dare let the driveway get to where he couldn't get out on the main road. Something might go wrong with Sophia or Georgie. He guessed they could manage their car once on that road, not that the county road grader was going by more than once a day on it. Hang it, if there was an emergency, he'd be pushing snow with his blade on the tractor all the way to town!

He dipped the shovel in the snow and scooped up a spadeful. He imagined the snow must be closer to two and a half feet now. The piles along the sides of the path resembled walls, and it was getting harder to toss the white stuff over them. He could see his breath, coming out in big icy puffs that looked like smoke.

He must remember to scoop up some of the clean snow from the yard and take it inside. Sophia had told Georgie she would make him some snow ice cream.

Maybe all this snow would make the soil need less irrigation next spring. It had been difficult to pay the water bill on time for watering the crops last fall. He hadn't been able to get the crops sold at the price he'd hoped they'd bring. But then, they'd been warned by the government that the first year wouldn't yield as well as those coming afterwards. And, it had made him feel very, very proud to get his first check for growing a crop on his own land!

Jack stopped his heaving of the shovel to catch his breath. He'd heard that even hale fellows had heart attacks sometimes from shoveling snow in weather like this.

They wouldn't be going to church today. Probably John's family wouldn't get there either, and would understand why Jack and Sophia and their son hadn't come by for dinner after church, as they'd been invited.

Sophia had stayed optimistic that they'd be able to accept their neighbors' invitation, and had baked a great-smelling cherry pie last night. They'd be enjoying that wonderful cherry pie with whip cream today.

Whoops! Looked like the lights just went off in the house. That would mean the electricity had gone out again. He'd have to dig some logs out of the wood pile and carry them in to use in the old stand-by wood burner. He finished the path, and began to dig his way towards the wood pile. He was able to lift up several logs and still carry the shovel over his shoulder as he made his way back to the house.

Jack was quick to pull the door shut behind him, attempting to keep the cold air from sweeping through the house. Georgie raced to meet him.

"Daddy, daddy, the 'lectricity is off!" Georgie was proud to bear the news. Sophia was looking through the junk drawer for the candles they kept for these occasions.

Jack noticed that Sophia still wore her blue plaid housedress with the belt tightened around her waist. He knew this wouldn't be the case for long. Her pregnancy would soon begin to show. At least she seemed to continue to feel well!

Jack began to pull off his outer clothes and hang them from the hooks by the door.

"Well, Georgie, looks like we're going to be staying home today and playing like we are pioneers." Jack glanced over the boy's tousled hair into Sophia's gaze.

She drew in a breath and managed a smile. "Looks like we'll be celebrating our big storm with cherry pie."

Georgie caught the spirit of excitement and clapped his hands, laughing. "Daddy, will you teach me to play dominos?"

"I expect so, son." Jack smiled as he helped Sophia position the candles around the kitchen, lighting them each carefully with wooden matches from the matchbox. "You stay a long ways off from these candles. They can burn you badly, and could also burn the house down!"

Georgie was pulling a chair over to the window so he could climb onto it and attempt to peer out to see the snow coming down. However, he couldn't see through the frozen ice on the bottom portion of the window. Sophia went over to her small son and used her apron to wipe the window above the iced area. She lifted her son high so he could see the white, whirling snow. Sophia set the child back on his feet as she stood looking wistfully through the window.

"I wonder what John and Charlotte are doing about now," Sophia murmured. Jack knew it was hard for her to give up the longed-for companionship they'd planned for the day.

"Shoveling snow would be a fair bet," Jack muttered.

*   *   *

"One of these days, we'll all have telephones out here, Charlotte." John came up behind his wife and gave her a hug as she took the spare plates from their table.

The "good" tablecloth, with the green ivy embroidered around the edges, still had its crisp folds from the iron. "Then, when we have to cancel plans, we can all phone each other."

"That sounds like a fairy tale, Hon." Charlotte smiled wistfully into John's kind brown eyes. She carefully placed the clean dishes and silverware back into their cabinet. "At least we'll have plenty of left-over roast beef."

"I'd better go out and break the ice for the cow trough," said John, pulling on his winter coat. He positioned his earmuffs and pulled the stocking cap over his head. He reached for the doorknob with his leather-gloved hand.

John used the scoop shovel to push the latest snow down what now resembled a tunnel, with snow piled high on either side of the path to the shed and to the outdoor toilet. He dug the snow away from the outhouse door and made a quick, chilly stop. T'was time to bring out some more catalogues. There would be no spiders weaving their webs in the corners where the rough walls met the ceiling for awhile. Probably would be a relief to Kevin, who sometimes worried that a spider or snake would poke its head up through that toilet hole and bite his bottom.

Hitching his clothes up again, John pulled his gloves back on and once again went about the business of clearing the snow from the narrow path to the cow shed. He brought down his to trusty sledgehammer smartly onto the ice on the cattle water trough to break it through. He pulled the pieces of ice from the surface of the trough and the cows moved to put their noses into the chilly water. A wee icicle was hanging from one cow's chin. Amazing, he thought, what animals could endure.

He stopped at the truck, climbed aboard, and started the engine. A shame to waste gasoline, but a guy had to keep starting the engine every other hour or so to keep it from freezing up so the vehicle could be operable in case of an emergency. At least these freezing-cold winters gave them a break from worrying that it would be a snakebite which was the emergency.

Banging the truck door shut, with the engine roaring reassuringly, John again began to scoop the path clean back to the house. He wondered how the neighbors, the Zanders, were getting along in this blizzard. That Henry was a nice enough guy and his wife, Flora, seemed to have lots of spunk. But there was just something kind of sad that seemed to hang over them and that baby girl of theirs.

*   *   *

"Henry, Henry!" Flora shook Henry's shoulder. He smelled foul, sour from the beer of the night before. "Henry, it's nearly noon. Wake up. I need you to dig us out. We're having a storm." There'd been no rousing him earlier.

Flora had already been out to milk the cow, since little Patty had been asleep after her early morning nursing. But, it had been very difficult to force the front door open far enough to reach the shovel and begin to dig. She hated the cold snow!

"Come on, Henry. You brought me to this God-forsaken country. Now, get up and be a part of it!" Flora's tears were warm against her cool cheeks; she could see her breath in the air.

The electricity had been off for an hour now, and it was cold throughout the house except for the kitchen, where Flora had the oven door propped open. The propane gas stove wouldn't do much but keep the worst of the chill off. She had Patty in extra blankets in her bassinet near the oven.

"Henry!" If she got any louder, she'd wake the baby. Not that the poor infant hadn't had to listen to loud quarreling before. Henry said she started all their fights. It seemed like Henry had drunk more when she was in the hospital having the baby and just wouldn't slow it down again afterward. She tried not to be a fussy wife, but sometimes it was all just too much.

"Ohhh ... my head. What is all the shouting about?" Henry was moving about under the covers at last. He turned his head and pulled his be-whiskered chin from under the blankets. "Hey, Honey." He was smiling! He dared to smile at her!

"We are having a blizzard. I can't leave the baby to go out anymore. I need you to help out here."

Henry sat up, holding his head. "Why's it so cold in here?"

"The power's off. Must be the storm. I can't get out long enough to dig out the woodpile. We really need to fire up the wood-burning stove in the living room. I'm just using the oven." Flora was trying to be matter of fact and not accusatory in her tone.

Henry pulled his jeans on over his long underwear, grabbed his flannel shirt from the nearby chair, and pulled on his boots. "What time is it?"

Flora swallowed back what she really thought–that it was way too late for a gentleman to be getting up–and managed to say calmly, "It is near noon."

Henry had the decency to look surprised and maybe a little guilty. He went to the cupboard and pulled out a box of corn flakes. Going to the icebox, he reached for the milk, but pushed it back. His handled settled on a beer bottle.

Flora wanted to scream. Was it going to start all over again so soon today? She forced patience. "Dear, you're going to need your breakfast. It is too cold outside to be out there working without some decent food in your belly."

He put the bottle back. "Just kidding, Sweet Thing. Can you bring me a dish for the cereal?"

Patty awakened and began to whimper and Flora handed Henry a bowl and a spoon on her way to gather up the baby.

"It worries me to have all these blankets so close to the oven. I'm afraid we'll catch the poor baby on fire." Flora spoke to her husband as though he was a partner who cared about her feelings. She didn't know if he truly did, anymore.

"I'll be out to dig out the logs here shortly. Is the cow still needing to be milked?"

"No. I got to her while the baby slept. And I don't think the snow was nearly so deep yet. But, it was quite a trick to get the front door open, with the snow drifted against it."

Again, Henry looked a bit remorseful. Perhaps he did care. Maybe he just acted like he didn't when he was drinking. She didn't know. She'd once heard that the things people say when drunk are the things they really mean. She hoped not. He had called her a "bitch" last night. He'd said his mother had warned him that she was "nothing but a bitch." The cruel words had cut deeply, as she'd been treated very nicely by Mr. and Mrs. Zanders, and they'd once told her she was "just what Jackie needs." Was she a fool to love his parents?

As Henry pushed out the door, Flora drew a sigh of relief and began to find herself hopeful they could have a pleasant day together. She seated herself in the rocking chair she'd pulled near the stove and began to nurse Patty.

"You are an angel. Just a sweet, little precious angel." Flora began to sing to the baby the song she'd created as their nursing song. "Eat up, my Darling. You have lives to bless."

She drew the baby from beneath the shawl she'd cast over her breast and slid her shirt back in place. She placed the bundled baby over her shoulder and began to pat her tiny back. She walked to the window and looked out to see how Henry was doing with his shoveling. The snow came to above Henry's knees. He was throwing the snow like the strong young man he was. He was able to make much better time than she had earlier in the day, and the snow wasn't so deep then, either.

This was supposed to be a sweet time in their lives, a new baby and a new start in this little log house. But, it was getting to be downright unpredictable.

The burp past, Flora seated herself and continued to nurse from her other breast. She probably could have fed five babies, with all the milk the good Lord had supplied to her. Patty was nuzzling away happily under her little pink blanket and Flora could feel her own nose getting cold.

It sounded like Henry was kicking at the door. Flora placed the snoozing baby in her bassinet, covered her well, and hurried to the door.

Henry's arms were full of frosty logs, losing some snow, as he placed the pile inside on the floor. "We'd better close the door fast! It's dratted cold out there!" He stomped his feet once more and moved inside, as Flora closed the door. The room was now colder than ever.

"This is one of those storms we've heard about." Henry was pulling his boots off and the snow-covered coat, too. "An old timer told me once out here that he'd driven across five-foot-high snow drifts!"

He picked up several of the logs and moved to the living room, where he knelt to place them in the wood burner in the middle of the room. Flora hurried to take from its top the artificial flower arrangement she'd kept there to try to make it more attractive, since they now had such a nice electric heater. Which, of course, was turning out to be quite worthless in an electric outage.

Henry stood up and reached out to hug Flora. "We're going to have a warm house in no time, now. You look very pretty in that red dress …"

Flora hadn't felt pretty tucking the red dress into a pair of slacks so she could milk the cow earlier. But Henry did know how to help a woman feel like a woman.

"What say we duck into the bed and get warm together while the house is heating up?" Henry was flirting with her; obviously he didn't remember the mean, cutting words he'd wounded her with just last night.

"I have a better idea. Why don't you cut the ham? I can place a couple slices in the oven now that I can close its door. It's time for lunch and we can enjoy it without a baby on my lap!"

CHAPTER 22

The Leperous Land

"JOHN, I SEE something happening on that south section of your field that doesn't look so good." Jack placed one hand on his neighbor's shoulder and pointed across the green oat field that was swaying in the light July breeze.

John nodded and took off his hat to run his fingers through his thick hair. "I've been hoping it would somehow be okay. But it's getting worse, Jack. No matter how much or how little I irrigate it, it just seems that piece of land won't drain right. Look at how it's getting all white across the top."

"Seems it might be a good idea to contact the Bureau of Reclamation to have some of those drains built into the ground down that way," John continued. "But I hate to have all that equipment tearing up my fields. Guess if it fixes it, it might be worth it in the long run. But, Jack, who knows how much the repayment will be for all this seep repair that is starting to creep across our homestead project?"

"Well. It's 1952 now and we will have eight more years, according to the agreement we signed when we came, before we begin to repay for any construction. I think we're getting pretty good at getting a feel for taming this wild land. You are no shabby farmer, my friend." Jack searched to find some way to ease the disappointed expression on his friend's face.

"Sounds so corny, but sometimes I think I've come to downright love this patch of dirt that's my very own." John's voice held a desperate tone. "I have to believe the government was truthful to us when this land was represented to us to be 'of a quality to provide an adequate living ...'"

"I don't know," said Jack, his own face drawn with seriousness, "I ran into another homesteader at the store in Pavillion yesterday who is hoppin' mad. He claims he brought his family out here to Wyoming for just a bunch of empty promises!"

John turned and scrutinized Jack's face. "You mentioned 'taming the wild ground.' To me, this ground is a bit like a bucking bronco! And I might get bucked off a bit, but I'm staying put until I get this wild land settled clear down!"

"Me, too." Jack grinned. "I'm in it for the long run. Maybe little Georgie will be the farmer on that land of mine one day. Besides, they're talking about letting us have double the 160 acres we started with. Guess the ones who are abandoning their sections are going to be leaving some land for those of us who don't give up so easily."

A tractor putt-putted in the background and a whippoorwill sang from somewhere across the ditch. The two sun-baked men stood quietly, side by side.

"So, guess I'd better get the water changed out in the corn field. Corn's supposed to be knee high by the Fourth of July. And look, here it is the fifteenth and my corn's quite a bit higher than my knees. If nothing else, our families can eat plenty of canned corn over the winter!" John chuckled and headed for the tractor, where his shovel rested against a huge ribbed rubber tire.

Jack smiled and waved and headed for his own vehicle, parked behind John's tractor. Under the smile, disappointment tore at him. He had expected challenges on his homestead land. But, he'd never dreamed that there would be huge, ugly concrete culverts strewn about the homesteaders' properties. Nor could he have imagined the obnoxious, obtrusive sounds of his soil being dug away in preparation of forming drains to carry away excess salts and water.

CHAPTER 23

A Breath Of City

A T A DISTANCE, the forward and backward motion of the heavy equipment sounded out a steady rhythm of loud growls and grunts. Flora drew in a deep breath, savoring the scent of sweet clover. Patty must have, also, because she sneezed twice, and then brought her little fist to her eyes to rub them.

"What's the matter, Honey? Do you have hay fever?" The young mother reached down and used her hanky to wipe the toddler's nose.

Patricia moved her head back and forth in disapproval over the cloth pushed against her nose.

She brightened and pointed to a yellow butterfly sitting on the tray of her baby carriage. "Ya..Ya..Da."

Flora laughed, tossing her curls. "I'm sure you just said 'butterfly!' Uh-oh, when you tried to touch it, you scared it away. See, it's flying off now."

Flora pushed the carriage to the car and managed to get the child into the front seat. She rolled down Patricia's window just a couple inches and carefully closed the door. Opening the back door, she struggled a bit as she folded the carriage and placed it into the backseat. Patty was standing up, holding onto the back of the seat when Flora opened the driver's door and slid in under the steering wheel.

"You must be a good girl and sit down now, Sweetie!" Flora turned the child and pulled her little feet out in front of her so she sat down soundly upon the ruffled panties that covered her rubber pants.

Flora started the engine and backed the car out of the driveway.

"We're going to Riverton to get some canvas for daddy. He needs the canvas for new dams. We're also going to get another shovel, because Mommy may have to start irrigating, 'cause daddy doesn't always finish his work." Flora knew she was just sharing her thoughts out loud, using a soothing tone to keep the child interested in the long trip to town.

"We are going to buy some chickens, because Mommy needs to make sure we have enough to eat when winter comes again. And maybe we will find some bushels of peaches to can, too."

"Da Da. Da Da."

"You think so, huh? Well, me too! I think Daddy should take better care of us. But, I don't know what's wrong. Maybe he has too many bad memories from when he was in the military. I can't imagine what it would be like to live with memories of killing people in the war ..."

Flora handed her daughter a dolly with a zipper shirt so the child could be busied for awhile zipping and unzipping the front of her doll.

To the sound of the zipper and the child kissing and crooning to her baby, Flora pondered the situation at her house this morning. Henry was drinking more often than not these days. Sometimes she could get him out of bed and remind him of the day's tasks. Often, he would leave the fields before the day's work was done and head towards Pavillion. She was certain he was going to the bar, and wasn't sure how they would continue to afford such a thing. She had seen him digging in the piggy bank that Patty's great-grandma had sent to Patty when the baby was born. True, she'd hidden the bank after that; but it was disconcerting to see Henry putting his beer ahead of his family. He didn't always say hurtful things to her when he'd had too much to drink, but she was finding herself getting a stress headache these days waiting for the verbal abuse to erupt when he was drinking.

Flora stopped at the Pavillion post office, dropping off the package she'd prepared for her sister's birthday. She hoped the pillow cases she'd made would be as welcome for Shirley as the little gifts she received from her sister always were. Sometimes those little notes from home were the bright spots of some very bleak days.

She laid the wiggling Patricia down on the car seat to change her diaper as she placed the child back in the car. The little girl really had been quite good for the first part of their little trip. She placed the little blonde head on her lap and gave her daughter a bottle as she drove on toward Riverton.

She applied the brakes as the car wound around Dead Man's Curve. She saw it as a fitting name for the black-topped road with its drop-off on one side and butting against a hill on the other.

Steering with her left, Flora wriggled her free arm under the knees of the youngster and pulled the sleeping child off her lap. She took the empty bottle from Patty's lips and propped it next to the little girl. She moved her shoulder, trying to work the kink out of it. Now, it wouldn't be so awkward to steer.

It took an hour to get to Riverton. She only passed two vehicles on the way. In this farming community, everyone was busy in the fields on a nice day like this. She could see hay being cut, and hay being baled in the fields along the way. There were long stretches of road where there was nothing but dirt and sagebrush, with no fences alongside. These were the places where the winter blizzards would blow the drifts across the roads and make traveling so perilous.

Patty began to stir as Flora entered town. "Hey, Sweetie. You are such a good little girl. Wake up. Look at the big city!" Patty sat up on her knees and peered out the side window. "Well, maybe not such a big city, but the biggest town you'll see for awhile."

Flora pulled onto the street in front of the J.C. Penney store, rolling down her window and craning her neck to make sure that she got the car parallel-parked properly. Rolling up her window, she cautioned the toddler to be patient, as Flora went to the back seat to get out the carriage and set it down on the pavement. Her heart was instantly cheered as she listened to the bustle of life in town. She placed her baby girl in the carriage and placed the diaper bag behind her.

"No, Honey. Dolly stays here." Flora smiled at Patty's cries of "Bay Bay!"

Wow! There was a lovely red and white dress in the store window. The strawberries woven into the fabric were accented by embroidered strawberries on the collar and pocket. And the red buttons down the front were just the right finishing touch. Perhaps she could get a bolt of fabric and make herself and Patty matching dresses!

As she pushed the door open and entered the store, Flora breathed in the air of the new fabrics and the floor polish on the wooden floor. Drinking beer might be the "fix" for her husband, but coming back to the civilization of town was very nearly a "fix" for her.

Returning home was not as pleasant a ride as the one into town. Even though she'd taken the little girl to the park in Riverton and pushed her on the baby swing before they had a picnic lunch, Patricia had fussed and cried much of the ride home, wanting her momma to hold her.

Although she had resorted to seating Patty on her lap and letting her help steer, it had become too much of a hazard, and she'd had to set the child beside her with an arm around her.

These trips were much better taken when a husband and wife could both be along. Ah, well. Life wasn't perfect.

As she pulled into the drive, Flora could see that Henry's pickup truck was still gone. Hopefully, he was finishing up some work in the field and had not headed to the bar again.

It was nearing dark, and dang it! She could see the cow standing in the corral, waiting to be milked. It was going to be one more struggle, trying to have Patty sit in the carriage while she milked the cow. And how Flora hated it when the flies tried to land on the little girl!

Flora pushed the child in the carriage to the house, and quickly changed into the overhauls she'd begun to wear when she did the milking. She took last night's stew from the icebox and placed it into the oven, turning it to 300 degrees. She changed Patty's diaper again, tossing the wet one, along with the one in the bread wrapper bag, into the foul-smelling diaper pail.

Now, with Patty sucking on a hard baby cookie, Flora could push her carriage to the barn, with the milk bucket and clean rags in the back compartment.

"See the cow, Patty?" Flora was determined this baby should have a good life. She kept her tones cheerful for the wee one.

"Hey, Flo, let's get you more comfortable." She placed a cup of oats into the trough and opened the barn door to the corral, letting the cow approach to slide her head into the stanchion, which closed with a snap. Flora waved a fly from the cookie of the watching child before she pulled out a stool and straddled it near the cow. She pushed against the cow's back leg, and the cow compliantly stepped back on that hoof, so that the bulging udder was exposed. Flora pulled the wet rag from the bread wrapper bag in her pocket and washed down the cow's teats and the surrounding udder area. She reached over and pulled the bucket underneath the cow, and began the ping-ping of milk streaming into it.

Patricia was crying angrily over her dropped cookie and a fly was sitting on the child's curls when Flora finally finished emptying the cow of her milk. Flora knew better than to try to comfort her daughter before letting the cow out. She quickly got a broom and swept out the cow dung the cow had trod in on her hooves.

At last, she could set the foaming milk bucket into the carriage and begin to sing loudly to Patty as she pushed her to the house.

Still no pickup truck in the drive. Oh, well, she could feed and bathe Patty and maybe relax a bit before the nightmare began tonight.

CHAPTER 24

What's His Plan?

CHARLOTTE'S HEAD ACHED. She and John had been up late last night. Though they'd gotten the kids to bed at a good time, it had been a night when John needed to talk. He and Charlotte had stepped outside onto the path to the driveway for a rare walk. He'd been pacing back and forth in the moonlight near the growing structure that was actually starting to look a lot like their new house.

"Here we are, coming closer to getting into our real house and out of that one-room shack. And, it's beginning to look like the land won't really support our family."

Charlotte had alternated between walking beside him and standing still, letting him pace around her. Her legs seemed to tire sooner than his. From time to time, she had murmured sympathetic sounds, but knew he really mostly needed a good listening to.

John's forehead had been furrowed. His hands running through his hair left it sticking up in every direction. "Jack and I were talking today. We both can see how much of the farmland is getting soggy. Less ground can be farmed than we thought. It's hard to get into some of the halfway decent fields with all that drain work going on down there all summer. The FHA keeps needing most of our money for payments; and, Hon, I see you putting cardboard in the bottoms of your shoes to make them last longer …"

Charlotte had heard the pain in his voice. She had been very touched; John wasn't given to noticing the little things. She had gone to him and stood close, reaching up to enclose his cheeks in her hands.

"John. This is our home. You are gentling the ground. We will make it work. I don't need fancy shoes right now. I have a good church pair, and I can use the overshoes if it comes to that, for us to stretch the grocery money a bit. We are not going to quit. You'll finish this house, and we will invite the neighbors in for a house-warming potluck!"

He had hugged her so tight, and swung her around in the moonlight, that her braid had fallen down from where she had it pinned up in the back. They had talked on into the night, until it was their slapping at mosquitoes that reminded them they had a comfortable bed waiting. The children had still been asleep when they slipped back into their one-room cabin.

*   *   *

Charlotte took down the bottle of aspirins from the medicine closet nailed onto the Celotex wall. She shook out a couple and swallowed them with a glass of water.

What she really needed was a good talk with Sophia. Let's see, Kevin would not be home from school for another hour and a half. She would call the children in from outside and take them to Sophia's for a bit.

Sophia was deftly removing the laundry from her clothesline when Charlotte drove up the drive. Deirdre ran to play with Georgie, while Charlotte hitched baby Gloria up on one hip and helped pull more of the dry clothes off the line.

"I'm surprised to see you today. But, it's good!" Sophia was smiling brightly at her unexpected guest. "Here. Just put those clothes into this basket. Your arms are full enough with little Gloria."

"Your baby asleep inside?" Charlotte jerked her head in the direction of the house.

"Yes. Let's go have a glass of Kool-Aid." Sophia turned her attention in the direction of the children, who were admiring Georgie's new trike. "Don't you kids be leaving the yard. The snakes are bad out just now."

As Sophia poured the purple Kool-Aid, and set out some oatmeal cookies, Charlotte settled Gloria on a blanket on the floor, then seated herself at the table.

"Sophia, is Jack worrying about how the farming is going?"

Sophia paused with her cookie close to her mouth. "Well. We know there's a committee trying to figure out what to do about the way the soil is turning out. I think it helps Jack to be able to talk to your John."

Charlotte leaned forward on her elbows. "Sophia. Do you worry?"

"I pray a lot, Charlotte. I cannot believe God allowed us to be the chosen homesteaders, only to have a dirty trick up His sleeve. And, I know we truly think so much of your family. It's as though we are relatives or something, by now. If we weren't all having to work so hard alongside each other, maybe we wouldn't be so close."

Charlotte swallowed back her tears, along with the knot that was forming in her throat. "You're right, Sophia. I'm so glad to have you as my friend. I suspect God is pretty busy sorting through all our requests. I think tonight I need to be sure that He hears I'm grateful for all the blessings, too."

A low cry, much like the sound of a kitten mewing, began to come from the bassinette in the hallway. Sophia moved to reach down and lift out the little bundle. "What's the matter? Did you wake up, Linda? Are you needing a clean diaper?"

Sophia deftly whipped a clean diaper from the pile under the bassinet and laid the wiggling bundle of pink blanket on the table to change the baby.

Even Gloria stopped rattling her rattle on the floor and scooted closer to see Linda, as Charlotte leaned over and allowed the baby to take her finger.

"I must go, Sophia. Kevin will be getting home on the school bus soon. I'll let myself out. Do you want me to send Georgie in?" She stooped and swept up Gloria, and turned to wave.

"Mommy, Georgie showed me the dead coyote." Dierdre's voice was full importance. "It's hanging in the barn."

"Humph. Thought we said to stay in the yard." Charlotte smiled down on Georgie. "Your mom needs you in the house. See you soon."

As Charlotte loaded the girls into the truck, she breathed in the late summer air. The smell of hay, and the sounds of tractors and balers. She could hear the frogs singing by the ditch. Sophia was right. This was a good home for them, and God was big enough to make everything turn out okay. Even her headache was better.

CHAPTER 25

Bad Breath

JACK WAS SO tired he could hardly move his shoulders enough to work the pain from the muscles across his upper back. He stepped slightly on the brake, and brought his vehicle slowly and carefully through the five-mile ravine. He wished a bridge would be built in that deep creek-bed soon. And, he wished he'd not run out of bailing twine today. Then he wouldn't have to be making this trip to Riverton for the string first thing this morning. He would lose a good two and a half hours of good, sunny baling weather.

It was beautiful outside today! To his right, he could see the canal bank which hid the irrigation water that gave life to this sun-baked land. To his left, he could see the huge sandstone rock that looked a bit like an eight-foot toadstool to the kids. And in its shadow, some pink primroses bloomed after the last summer shower. He drove with his sun-baked elbow propped out the open window, and listened to the sound of the shrilling birds from time to time. He was careful to keep his car tires from being grabbed by the deep ruts of the road.

What was that up ahead? Jack slowed the vehicle and started around the pickup truck that appeared to have gone off the wrong side of the road into the barrow ditch. He pulled his vehicle to the side of the road, careful not to mimic the other truck, which had one tire off the side right down into the ditch, forcing the truck to tilt. As he opened the car door and stepped onto the dirt road, Jack recognized the vehicle as Henry Zanders'. He wondered how the man had gotten home. As he strode closer to the pickup, he realized Henry was still inside.

Lord, what has happened here? He wondered, hurrying faster towards the driver's door. He could see his neighbor leaning forward, his face against the steering wheel.

Henry's window was up. He must have been here since last night. Finding the truck door unlocked, Jack opened it carefully and said, "Henry. Henry, my man. Are you hurt?"

The foul smell of beer met Jack's nostrils; he could see several beer bottles on the floorboard, along with a bag of spilled candies, no doubt for his little girl, waiting at home. Flora was probably worried sick.

Jack could see Henry's chest moving with his breaths. Afraid he could paralyze the man if his back or neck was damaged, Jack tried a louder approach. "Henry! Henry! Wake up. It's a snake!" Jack almost felt guilty.

Henry sat up straight and slowly moved his head to look at Jack in apparent confusion. "What? Snake? Where?" His eyes were bloodshot and his breath could compete with a skunk.

"You've had a wreck. Are you hurt, Henry?" Jack didn't answer about the snake.

"Oh … I think I'm okay. Let's see if I can get out of the truck." Henry's words were slurred. Jack steadied Henry with an arm around his shoulder as Henry lurched to the ground.

Henry began to laugh. "Look at me, Jack. Nothing wrong with me another beer wouldn't cure." He staggered a bit as he walked.

"Henry, do you remember what happened? How long have you been out here in your truck?"

"Well," Henry cast his eyes downward slyly, "I'd gone to Pavillion to get a few things … I think I left for home about eleven. What time is it?"

It was pretty apparent to Jack what those items were that Henry had been purchasing. "Henry, it's eight-thirty in the morning. You've been out here in the night for eight hours anyway. Flora is probably worried sick about you."

"Well, now, I bet you're right. Good thing I've taught her how to milk the cow."

Jack scratched his head. He was really sweating to get to Riverton and get back to his bailing before some summer shower came up. He couldn't afford to lose anymore time. Drat! If only there were telephones out here.

"Henry, I don't have any chain with me. Do you?"

"Let me look under the seat." Henry pulled the truck door open and bent down to gaze beneath the seat. "Nope. Don't guess you can pull me out. Want a beer?"

"No. And I think we'd better not have you drink anymore either for now because you're going to have to keep this vehicle on the road when you get her unstuck."

Henry pulled his hand back from where it had almost reached the remaining three beers in the pack.

Jack offered his plan. "I'm on my way to Riverton. I have to get some binding twine and get back to bailing my hay. I'll stop at the Ryssells' down the road and see if anyone is there who can pull you out or give you a ride back home instead."

Henry seemed to contemplate whether to take the beer or not, but got quietly into the green Ford with Jack.

They were quiet the next few miles as each held his own thoughts.

"You can wait here." Jack stepped out of the car and spoke through the open window to Henry. Then Jack reached in and took the keys, something he never did. He didn't want Henry to drunkenly decide to drive off, and he didn't want to take Henry in to worry the Ryssell woman if she was the only one there. But Jack was in luck. There was Gary Ryssell coming out the front door of the little tar-papered house.

"Hey, Gary. I'm in a real predicament. Henry Zanders is with me. I found his truck back there on the road a ways; he seems to have run it into the barrow pit last night. I don't have any chain to pull him out, and I'm desperate to get to Riverton and get some more binding twine so I can finish my bailing before it rains …"

"I can handle this, Jack." Gary was round, he had stubbles on his face, and his smile was wide. "I can't get to the fields today, anyhow. I'm waiting for a part for my combine. Might be in the mail later today. Why don't I take the Zanders fellow back with my chain and see what I can do?"

Jack blew out a breath of relief. "Thanks, Gary. Sometime, we should have you and the family over for a chicken dinner. Maybe further along towards winter, when the crops are in …"

Gary clapped the younger man on the back and rubbed his own unshaven cheek as they strode back towards Jack's car. "Sounds great. Let's do it."

Zanders appeared to be dozing as the two neared the car. Jack lowered his voice, "I think he got into too much old barley corn last night; I do hope he is safe to drive home."

"Hmmm. Well, guess I'll be gauging that as we ride along," Gary winked at Jack. "Hey, Zanders, wake up. I'll be helping you get your truck out of the ditch." He patted Henry's shoulder through the open window.

As Jack drove off, once again on the road for Riverton, he felt grateful he only had the regular problems in life. Then, he admitted to himself that he also felt disgusted. Henry Zanders ought to have been home milking his own cow last night and again this morning. His wife was really just a young city girl with a little baby. He now wondered what kind of life this was turning out to be for that young lady.

CHAPTER 26

Public Law 258

“**O**H, MY GOSH. They passed it as a new law.” Jack put his paper down and stared at Sophia in amazement. “Public Law 258 is the same as an admission that our land is faulty.”

“So, Honey, what does Bill 258 do for us when all is said and done?” Sophia didn't understand exactly what all the men had been talking about for the past few months.

“Well it says here that Public Law 258 passed on August 13, 1953, and it states that we can now have 320 acres of land per homestead farm, instead of 160 acres as was the previous law. Sophia, this is due to the government realizing the land we were granted is insufficient to provide for a family. It should have been enough to give us a good living. But all the seep land is cutting down production. And who knows how much more soil will seep out before we get ten years of farming in."

Sophia rubbed her rounded belly. She was beginning to think that maybe three kids would be enough. Jack had gotten her a new wringer washing machine now and that made washing the clothes take a bit less time, but the cloth diapers from her last two babies were being used for rags now. In a pinch, they'd worked well for sanitary napkins. She'd have to buy another couple dozen just to get by, with this new child due in January. The new safety pins wouldn't cost much, luckily, as her old ones were rusty, and sprung, too.

Sophia forced herself from the place she called her "little filly place." Just like a brooding mare, she could go inward, thinking only about babies. She shook her golden curls.

"Jack, that sounds like we can get twice the land we already have. Where does it come from?"

"Some of our neighbors are talking about leaving. They are tired of never knowing how much land will be good the next year. And they are tired of having nothing left over when they pay back their seed and water bill loans at the end of the year. Why, Gary Ryssell says he'd rather go back home and work in a grocery store than face his wife's disappointment again, after another skimpy harvest. I guess we could apply to add his land to ours."

"I'm surprised you don't say they're tired of the forty-below-zero winters here." Sophia murmured.

Jack looked up intently. "Hon, are you tired of the winters?"

Sophia's eyes misted. She could see that it would hurt his heart if she were unhappy here. "Honey, the winters are so fierce here. Of course, I get cold. And I always worry about you out shoveling and working in the cold. But, it mostly feels like an important part of this big adventure you've dragged me off on." Her smile lit up her face even though Jack still saw the tears glistening in her eyes.

He rose from the kitchen chair and knelt down on one knee in front of her. He hugged her tightly and whispered in her ear, "You are the most beautiful thing growing on this farm!"

Sophia secretly hoped the January weather would permit a hurried drive to town in order to deliver their next baby.

Georgie burst through the door and stopped so quickly that his sister, who had been racing behind him, ran right into his back. They both cried out with laughter. "Oh, look! They're hugging!" Georgie loved seeing his parents love each other.

"Come on! Hugs for everyone!" Jack held out his arms to his son and daughter. Sophia laughingly joined into the big circle hug.

Sophia found herself comforted that a double-sized farm might help them make ends meet a bit better next year.

CHAPTER 27

Beloved Traitorous Soil

JOHN'S FACE WAS streaked with brown dirt, and bits of hay stuck to his sweat-streaked felt Western hat. His mouth worked a twig of hay stubble that he had poking out between his lips. But Charlotte could see the happy gleam in his eyes as he stopped in front of her with a huge watermelon in his arms.

Charlotte stopped her sweeping of the front porch and laughed. "I was wondering if that melon wasn't about ready. I've seen you walking through the garden thumping it every day for awhile now."

John spat the hay stem from his mouth near the porch. "I'll put it down the well pit and let it cool. We can have it after supper tonight to celebrate more progress with this Homestead project."

He strode to the boxed-in topper over the well pit, and Charlotte watched him kneel and pull up the trap door on the box. He pulled up the rope and carefully wedged an end of the watermelon into the bucket hanging from the rope, lowering it with the care of a man who loved his watermelons. Charlotte knew this wasn't as handy as Sophia's icebox, but it worked out well, and didn't require a fee for buying blocks of ice in Pavillion.

She finished whisking the last bit of soil from the front porch as John again approached her, now smacking his hat against his thigh to drive out the debris attached to the felt.

She was smiling at John's delight over the melon as they entered the house. Some might think their new house rather simple, but Charlotte experienced joy each time she entered it and looked around. Three separate bedrooms allowed welcome privacy, and Charlotte thought her pretty blooming plants standing in front of the big picture window here in the living room added a nice touch.

John's purposeful steps took him straight to the sewing machine cabinet, where he rifled through the papers and pamphlets he had piled on top.

"Here, Charlotte. Listen to this. I think the Congress has to take our problem seriously now that B. E. Fogarty, C. R. Mairerhofer, and D. S. Mitchell have made their Water Resources and Power report:

'Of considerable concern is the question of the disposition of lands affected by canal and drainage problems, but of utmost concern is the social problem of the settlers whom we have permitted to settle on lands of unsatisfactory quality. The sufficiency of many of the farm units in the north Pavillion area and most of the units in the North Portal area is seriously questioned. It is extremely probable that within 10 years a majority of these farm units will lack sufficient irrigatable land to support a family. Lands which may be affected in the future pose the question of whether they should be forever subsidized or whether we should permit continued operation, realizing that many of the settlers on them will ultimately fail.'"

Charlotte drew a deep breath and sighed. She was proud of how her husband kept up so well on current events. And she knew he loved and respected this land the Lord had given them. But, sometimes she grew weary of him eating and breathing the political mess that had erupted out of the betrayal of the soil.

She recognized that John had reacted to her sigh and had jerked his head up from his reading, and with a cocked eyebrow and a grim jaw, was awaiting her response.

Charlotte moved across the floor and laid her hand on her husband's, which was gripping the stapled-together sheets of paper. "Honey, you are right. That is a powerful report. We'll keep praying that the right answers come so that our land can provide for this family."

John nodded, apparently satisfied with her answer. "You have the house looking good with these summer curtains up. We'll be working on turning the dirt yard into a lawn by next spring." His determination to continue to build a sturdy farm was his way of struggling against the white seep land that was showing not only on his land, but on many of his neighbors' by now. Thank goodness, his added parcel of 160 acres didn't yet show the soggy areas of his original tract of land.

His eyes moved to where Charlotte had been ironing and had temporarily hung some shirts on hangers from the top of the door. "You don't want to hang things from the tops of the doors, or even the door handles. That will spring the doors, and you remember how hard I worked to make sure they hung even."

He stepped to the clothes, and Charlotte held her breath, hoping he'd not wrinkle her work, as he carefully hung each one atop the door casing that ran across the top of the open door. "There. That won't hurt a thing. Say, Char, where are the kids?"

Now that everyone had their own place in this house to rest and relax, John found he no longer had little children racing to him when he entered the house. Oh, well, with every gain there is a loss.

"Kevin is still outside racing around with that dog we got him for his birthday. I think it's probably all right he didn't get the dog until he was nine! It seems he enjoys Shep in a way he mightn't have when he was younger. And Shep is so nuts about our boy, too. You know that dog is good with all of us, but Kevin is definitely his favorite! And the girls are playing house in their bedroom. Let's go peek; they're so cute …"

"Let me wash my face and hands first." John stepped into the open bathroom door and began to splash water on his face. Sure that he would spill onto her freshly scrubbed linoleum floor, Charlotte quickly handed him a washrag to finish his washing. She carefully closed the bathroom cabinet door. She cherished this house, with its fresh paint, after the cramped life in the Celotex-lined "chicken house."

Young female voices met their ears as they quietly moved down the hall towards the girls' room. As they opened the door, both parents smiled to see Deirdre dressed in Charlotte's old, long dress and Gloria dressed in Kevin's old clothes, both bending over the cat covered up in the doll buggy.

The girls turned at the sound of their father's escaped chuckle, and ran to give him a hug.

"We have a treat for after supper tonight, girls," he told them. "I'll gather up Kevin and we'll milk the cows while you finish supper," he added to Charlotte.

Now that they had four cows, it took longer for milking if only one person did it. Kevin was a bit slower than his father at the milking, but his hands showed a strength that belied his wiry stature.

Charlotte lifted the lid from a simmering pot and smelled the aroma of the ham and beans. Good thing a ham hock could be stretched for so long. She heard John's voice raised outside along the path, "Kevin, KEVIN! Time to milk the cows! …"

CHAPTER 28

Rattled

THE DARNED THING would have to get a flat tire just when she was desperate to go somewhere. Flora lifted her foot and stepped fully upon the jack handle, forcing it to turn one more time upon the nut on the wheel. If her Pennsylvania-bred mother could see her now, she'd be aghast. Probably Papa would be proud, though. He always thought her mama had pampered her too much.

She was lucky to have found a spare in the trunk that still held air. When she'd pulled it from the rear of the car, and bounced it on the ground, she'd found it to be sound. She doubted that Henry had checked on such things for the last year or so. And, she just couldn't remember to do everything.

Well, at least she'd seen the flattened tire before she got into the car, and she was still in her own driveway doing this tedious chore, instead of along the road for anyone to see.

Wrenching the jack handle one more turn, she got the nut loosened enough so she could now loosen all the bolts by hand. Squatting, she began to whirl the nuts, careful not to blemish her nail polish. She might be the only woman around here who still wore nail polish, but she was determined this land would not make her into a plain, ugly person. Probably she'd have to put on fresh lipstick and a spray of perfume when she finished with this greasy job!

Drat! Her dress hem was hanging in the dirt. She tucked it between her knees, careful not to get grease on it.

With a grunt and another powerful tug, the tire was off. Flora rolled it to the side as she reached for the inflated spare. What was that?!? She listened intently, focusing on some nearby sound over the call of the birds and the snap of the leaping grasshopper. The tractors droned in the distance.

"Ttttttt …" The blood drained from her face as every muscle in her body froze. There was a rattler nearby, and its rattle was warning her that it was ready to strike. With her body frozen into its half-kneeling posture, Flora didn't even turn her neck, as she cast her eyes about for the snake.

There! The tan and brown coil almost looked like a rope, except for its arched length with the quivering head, beady eyes gazing at her over its darting tongue. The rattler was about four feet away, right in front of the car; it had probably slithered out from beneath the vehicle.

Flora thought of her three-year-old daughter napping in the house. She needed her mother; Lord knew, she had a father that was next to worthless. Here it was one more night that Henry had not made it home. She'd given up wondering if he'd run his car into the canal in a drunken binge, and saw it as normal, now, that she couldn't depend on him. A woman couldn't live in constant worry, 24 hours a day.

Listening keenly to the "tttttt" of the rattler, Flora knew her options were limited. She must stay very quiet and hope the snake would slither away; the shovel was back at the house and she couldn't outrun a snake. The twenty-two rifle was loaded in the open trunk, but this front tire she'd been working on was too far from the trunk.

Lord, help me! Her cry was only within but it filled all of her, as she continued to half crouch, her muscles burning.

Slowly the snake drew in its darting tongue and lowered its head to the ground. In an almost elegant motion, it slowly swept its length away from Flora. Also in slow motion, the woman drew herself up to her full height and allowed her burning muscles to relax. Then, she slowly side-stepped to the trunk, never allowing the snake to leave her sight. She reached inside and lifted out the rifle, careful not to touch the trigger. The snake was still moving forward, almost to the nearby bushes. If it got to the bushes, it would slide from sight, and remain a peril to her family for another day.

Raising the gun, Flora looked down the sight and placed it squarely upon the rattler, drew in her breath, and held it while she pulled the trigger. As a crack split the air, the snake began to writhe, and Flora knew it had been hit but wasn't dead. She dropped the gun and raced to the house to get the shovel that leaned by the door. She ran towards the wriggling snake and brought the shovel's point down onto it with a sharp jab. She couldn't seem to stop herself; she kept bringing the shovel down again and again, until she realized the snake had been dead for some time.

She pushed the shovel under the rope-like body and carried it out to the road, throwing it into a rut. The vultures would get a treat, and maybe a passerby would skid on it and then add her snake's rattles to his own tally of conquered rattlesnakes!

Flora replaced the shovel by the door and went inside to soap down her hands, and try to rinse the bile from her mouth. She peeked in on sleeping Patty, glad to see the child would have a mommy for one more day, anyway.

It didn't take long for Flora to finish putting the spare tire on the car. She pulled open the screen door to go inside and wash her hands, freshen up her lipstick, and spray on some fresh scent. In the mirror, she noticed something she'd not really seen before. There was a grownup staring back at her.

"Mommy, I'm hungry." Little Patricia had climbed out of bed and come to the bathroom door.

Flora leaned over and picked the little girl up, holding her in a tight hug. "Hi, Mommy's Patty-Patty-Cakes. Let's have a hot dog and then go to the store in Pavillion."

"Why?" Flora had to smile at the expected response from her child. "Why" seemed to be her favorite word these days.

"Because it's Halloween, and we are going to get some treats for all those ghosts and goblins that will be coming to our door tonight." Flora smiled at her daughter's puzzled expression.

There had been a rare thunderstorm last night. It had rained enough that Flora didn't have to figure out if she should be out irrigating the crops. That was a relief. Her daughter was getting very heavy to backpack along with her in her papoose carrier; she'd be darned if she'd have the little one down near the ground as Flora stomped along in this snake-ridden countryside.

On her own feet again, the child attempted to skip as she followed her mother to the kitchen. She watched the wieners come from the refrigerator and land in the kettle of water on the stove. She helped her mom carry the bread and the ketchup to the table. Her mother was making some lemonade Kool-Aid, their favorite. And now she was opening a jar of canned applesauce. Patty carried her own Sears and Roebuck catalogue to the chair and climbed up on it as her mom finished making lunch. "Mommy, why do we eat dogs?"

Placing the steaming wieners on the hot pad, and the bowl of applesauce on the table, Flora nearly choked with laughter. "They aren't real dogs, Honey. That's just what we call them to be silly."

A sense of well-being settled upon Flora. Many wives out here no doubt would think today a dreadful one, with a missing husband again, and Flora suspected that even the most weathered farm wife might have been a little hysterical over the snake encounter. But Flora knew, with the reassurance of a giggling three-year-old, that her life would be okay.

CHAPTER 29

A Rescue Is Planned

"**T**HEY'VE ASKED JACK to run for the school board." John stood, looking intently at Charlotte, who was almost buried in all the pillowcases she was embroidering and tablecloths she had been crocheting for Christmas presents. The davenport appeared to be the only seat in their living room that wasn't covered.

Charlotte focused on what John was saying over the sound of the Christmas music emanating from the radio. "Jack? Well, he'd sure be a good board member. I can't imagine anyone not voting for him." She placed her finger on her thread and held her embroidery hoop still so as not to lose her place while she looked up at her husband.

He looked so handsome tonight. Christmas always brought out the best in everyone in this family. Besides, she guessed he was excited for his friend.

"Kids, stop calling each other 'stupid idiots!'" said John, with momentarily furrowed brow. The two older kids were quarreling over their Skunk dice game at the kitchen table. Gloria was ignoring all the sibling conflict, busy playing dolls under a tent she'd constructed by stretching a sheet from the davenport to the coffee table.

"Yes," John continued, "he should get the votes. I'll sure vote for him. The guy is pretty busy, though, trying to drive to Montana to take college courses a couple days a week. He says he's got to figure out some additional way to make a living since he was hit with those doubled-up leveling costs from when the extra 160 acres was added." John began to pace, one arm folded behind his back, gripping his other elbow. Charlotte could tell this was evolving into a serious talk, so she bent her head to continue her embroidering so she would be able to get these gifts mailed out in time.

"Adding another parcel of land was supposed to help this poor land provide a living. Doesn't seem right that we should be charged double now; just makes it harder financially … I am thinking we ought to join with the other farmers out here who are raising a dairy herd to make ends meet." John glanced at Charlotte to see if she was already going to raise a protest about adding on more to the loan. "Selling our little bit of milk and cream to neighbors has been a bit of a financial boost, but we are sinking fast here. Thank the Lord, this year we did get a bit left over after harvest, unlike last year when we had to give the whole profit to the FHA for our loan. And, then, to think: we were made to get that new piece of equipment, too. The old one could have been welded and worked out a bit longer."

Charlotte nodded.

"Did you hear me, Char?" John had stopped his pacing to stare at her.

Charlotte raised her head, nodded and said, "Yes, I heard you. Go on." She inwardly grimaced; she should know he needed an occasional grunt or "Oh, my" when he was on one of his rants.

"Well, we just have to generate more income. More and more of the fields are becoming bogs. I believe we'll be able to raise enough hay to keep a full dairy herd in operation. We might also grow the oats to entice them into the barn. We would have to pay to have the oats rolled. At least this part of the business would only have an initial start-up cost … twenty cows would begin to produce more cows soon enough."

"Twenty!" Charlotte gasped. "Good Heavens, John! How could you milk twenty or more cows two times a day? It's not humanly possible. And you still have all the farming to do, too. I know Kevin is a bit of help with the milking and the farming, but he has got to be able to participate in his school activities, too. They're talking about bringing football to the high school. He's really excited that there might be a sport that's right for him."

"Yes, I hope they get football here. We'll all go watch him play." John paced so quietly for a few moments that

Charlotte put her finger back on her embroidery work to hold her place and glanced up at him.

John's face wore his most determined expression atop his pacing frame. "I think we'll need to get automatic milking machines and one of those big cooled milk containers. We'll have to add on to the barn …"

Charlotte gasped. "John, how long would it take us to pay off a loan like that?"

John shook his head. "Not quite sure. But I'm going to put a pencil to paper and see. I think the milk income could be enough to get us out of this pit of debt that we can't seem to find a toehold to climb out of."

This serious turn of events was not quite enough to bring down Charlotte's bright Christmas mood, but it was dimming. "Honey, I see that you've put a lot of thought into this possibility. I know you are worried about our finances. You have me keep the farm books. It's such a struggle to even have enough for the kids' school clothes now. It is helpful that they are in 4-H, and that Deirdre has learned to sew her own clothes. Between the things she sews herself, and the ones I make her, and the hand-me-downs of your nieces back in Kansas, she's never had a store-bought dress!"

"See?" John was obviously feeling validated.

Charlotte was on a roll of her own. "I have saved the egg money all year to buy our Christmas this year. Every time I get a quarter for a dozen eggs that I sell to the store, I put a dime of it away. I must admit, it would be nice to not have to scrimp so much all of the time."

"Well, then. I'm going to figure out how much it would take to get this operation off the ground, and see if I can calculate how long it would take for this dairy portion to break even. By the way, I guess there's something the kids would like: the dairy truck that comes for the milk could also bring us some ice cream from time to time. That refrigerator we bought a couple years ago might come in quite handy!"

"Ice cream! Are you making ice cream, Mommy?" Gloria was out of her tent, proving the old adage once again to Charlotte, "Little pitchers have big ears."

"No, Sweetie. Daddy is making plans for someday."

John wasn't finished. "I think we also need to have a bull here with the herd as well. I'll make him a separate bull pen so that he doesn't get in with the young heifers while they are too young and endanger them in the birthing."

"And, I've been thinking, Char. Now that there's one television channel that can make it across the mountains to us, it might be time for us to buy a television set. The neighbors have been mighty nice to invite us over to watch their new television. I love when we go there and watch the 'Gary Moore Show.'" I especially like that big-mouthed girl!" John laughed aloud.

"Carol Burnett. Her name is Carol Burnett, Dear." Charlotte stifled her own laughter. "And I also enjoy when we all watch the show 'I've Got a Secret' together. Now, where would we get the money for a television set? And those tall antennas for the top of the house must cost plenty, too?"

"I'm thinking we might do it all in the same transaction." John had stopped his pacing and, with growing confidence, carefully seated himself on the davenport across from Charlotte. He didn't want to unsettle that brick replacing a sofa leg. Because his wife hadn't stopped him earlier with a "We better pray about it first," she must be hearing the reason of what he was saying.

CHAPTER 30

The Mastery of the Land

JOHN HAD NEVER seen his friend Jack so upset.

Grabbing his cap from the ground where he'd tossed it with a loud "Damn!" Jack slapped the cap once more on his knee before setting it back on his tousled brown hair. "I mean it, man; what do they expect of us? You can't squeeze blood from a turnip! All that reconstruction work was done to fix the drainage problem and our lands are still seeping out. Not to mention those dratted drains running across our lands until even the livestock are stuck and dying in them! And look here, now they are talking about us having to repay all that reconstruction work to the tune of six million, three hundred thousand dollars! I've figured it out and if you look at the cost per acre, it would take us each 440 years, damn it, YEARS, to pay them back for that reconstruction!"

"Good grief!" John's face was not as red as Jack's at this point, but it was also deeply furrowed. "That would mean our kids and grandkids and their grandkids would all be the same as indentured servants to this land, to our government. And what would they have to repay with? More and more alkali bog land growing less and less harvest! And it's not as if there's anything left to pay for reconstruction—mine's all gone to the farm loans as it is!" John was pacing now, his elbow gripped behind his back. Whippoorwills were making the only sound in the tense silence.

Jack raised his chin and stared out across his cornfields. The sun was beginning to go down and the dusk was casting shadows from his fence posts. From this view, the horizon no longer showed a desolate land, but one that appeared to have been mastered by the farmer, ears of corn waving atop their proud stalks, and even a carefully planted tree silhouetted against the skyline. But Jack knew it was only an illusion. Turning in another direction, he would see the land showing its own mastery, vomiting up the white crust of salt across what were once his hard-worked fields, too.

"John, we've been able to grow this crop this year by using "extensions" for watering. But that's no solution. We can't continue to be held hostage to the threat that the water will be shut off if we don't agree to some outlandish repayment plan. We need a permanent settlement of this issue."

John stopped his pacing, and leaned over and yanked a stem from a nearby plant to thrust between his teeth.

"Actually, I am still thinking about the generations of our families that could be stuck with severe financial problems because you and I were determined to be homesteaders. The truth is, Jack, I don't see Kevin chomping at the bit to get his chance to work this land. He sees how hard it is for us, and he has seen his mother's tears as she's reached in the cellar for the last can of fruit she'd put up. I don't think our kids are stupid enough to want to follow in our footsteps …"

Jack turned and peered at his friend in the dimming light. Was John's voice actually growing husky? Jack chose his words carefully. "Friend, the kids aren't us. We were the homesteaders, choosing to set out on a fine adventure, an opportunity to turn this dirt and sagebrush into farmland. The government made a promise to us that the land would be sufficient for our families. You know how we had to meet all those conditions with the government in order to qualify to break this land. And we met all their conditions. We were military men, having seen hard battle, and we were ready to turn that battle against the rattlesnakes of Wyoming. And Lord knows, we killed plenty of rattlers those first few years!"

He chuckled and went on, "Our kids don't see this as the beckoning land we saw. They see it as the dirt that beats up mom and dad. They see it as the soil that comes shackled with government repayment plans, and bills that can never be paid. Hell, your son sees it as making him get up early in the morning to go to school while stinking like dairy cows. Maybe our kids will all move to town, and use their adventuresome spirit to fight their own battles in the city!"

John drew closer to his neighbor and confidante, a strong edge to his tone. "Well, I think it is important that our children see not only that we fought the enemy in war, but that we fought a valiant battle with this harsh land, and maybe they also need to see us ready to fight our very government in order to right this wrong! Our own government misrepresented our land to us!"

Jack sighed, "I know. It does seem that there's been purposeful deceit in how all those showy maps and land analysis reports were created to bring settlers to this land. According to what I've read, a guy named J. T. Whistler came here as early as 1916 to take soil samples, and two others came a year later to conduct more tests. Then a fourth man, named Harper, came in 1925, and, John, the authorities should not have ignored all four of those men when this land was considered for an irrigation project! Even that long ago, all four men were of the same opinion–that irrigating this land would eventually prove to be no good ..."

"I've been reading the same things. We will have to continue this talk. But right now I suspect that Charlotte is starting the milking and wondering where I am. When we started our dairy operation, I really thought I'd do most of the milking, with all the new-fangled equipment, but with Charlotte and me working together, it takes us two hours to knock out the milking. Kevin or the girls can sometimes help, but they're busy with their school functions ..."

As Jack climbed onto his Allis Chambers tractor and started the engine, John stepped quickly over the ditch and climbed with practiced expertise up over the barbed-wire fence, dropping to the ground near where his own truck was parked.

John started his truck and shifted into first gear with his mind in another place. During his drive home he couldn't stop remembering scenes from all these years of fighting with the land. He recalled the year that the aphids were eating up the alfalfa; he was one of the farmers that brought in boxes and boxes of ladybugs to spread over the crops to eat the aphids. To this day, he always grins when the occasional lady bug lands on a child's hand, and the child blows upon it, reciting, "Lady Bug, Lady Bug, fly away home. Your house is on fire and your children are alone."

And he remembered the many times that other insects had attacked, and how the crop-dusting planes had come to spray insecticide upon his fields. His mind moved over the details of how the neighbors had gotten together to help each other, waving white tee shirts at the corners of the fields so the pilot would know where to spray. As though it were yesterday, he could hear the sound of the plane dropping altitude overhead as he ducked and ran from the spray.

And the snow. The cold. The wretched north winds. The kids, stranded at school during a blizzard. And no phones out here yet to find a way to get them help.

Charlotte had been beside herself that time. She had just imagined the kids waiting at school with no one to come get them. But John had called on her faith and told her God always provided a way. And sure enough, some kind administrator of the school had driven them home across the snowdrifts in his jeep. John found himself smiling. That was the blizzard that took out the electricity for two of their milkings. Other students had ended up spending the night at Jack's place and all of the boys joined together to help milk the forty cows by hand. Everyone had been real interested in that big breakfast the girls had made over the butane-gas range!

As he reached his own driveway, John smiled at the irony. It seemed that this repayment threat was sounding an ever-heightening alarm, but they'd been here long enough now that his family finally had a telephone, even if it was just a party line serving eight homes, identified with short and long rings. It was really a great thing, especially if livestock needed a veterinarian. Of course, the girls loved talking to their friends, even though the neighbors might be listening in. Time was passing, and some things were progressing, even while the original problems just continued to grow.

The lights glowed brightly from the windows in the house, but he went directly to the barn, as those lights were glistening, too.

CHAPTER 31

A Date to Remember

"COME ON, BABY," said Henry, his voice nearly wheedling. He lowered his balding head to peer into Flora's snapping dark eyes. "We can get one of John and Charlotte's girls to watch Patty so we can spend an evening out. Let's plan to go to the drive-in movie. It's our anniversary, and I think it's time for us to put the hard work aside for an evening."

Flora continued her work in the garden, hoeing the meddlesome weeds from her cultivation rows. She couldn't quite figure out why Henry was so determined to spend an evening together having fun. He was probably trying to make up for having once again broken the promise that he was going to quit drinking.

To give him credit, she had, last month, watched him try harder than ever. She had gone to bed and forgotten to put away a letter she'd been writing to her sister in Kentucky. Henry had come home from an evening of drinking and somehow found the focus to sit down and read the letter that had been lying there on the kitchen table. He'd gotten an earful, because she had been honest with her sister regarding the past year, pleading that Shirley not tell her parents the situation she was in.

In that letter, she'd shared how Henry stayed out all night at times, and that she hoped he had some other woman he sleeps with, and even that syphilis symptoms might be his fate that would finish him! She had also disclosed that syphilis would not be a danger to her, that their intimacy had ended years ago; and Henry didn't even seem to notice the loss.

My! Henry had been nasty when he pulled her from the bed and ripped the letter to shreds in front of her. He'd told her that he did indeed notice how his bed had turned cold. Then, he'd blamed her "frigidity" as the cause for his excessive drinking.

Somehow, she'd found her voice and told him that he was nothing but a drunk and that she hadn't married a drunk, and didn't intend to stay married to a drunk. She'd taken some blankets to the sofa and spent the night in the living room. He'd slammed their bedroom door so loudly, she'd expected Patty to emerge from her own room with questions. Thankfully, that had not happened. The next morning, Henry had come out and found her blankets stacked neatly on the sofa, and seemed to recall much of what had occurred the night before.

He had come up behind where she was frying bacon and wrapped his arms around her, his receding red hair snuggled down on her dark, uncombed hair. His voice was gruff, and his breath was worse than a dragon's when he stated, "Honey, I promise you. I am not drinking anymore. You can look in the refrigerator, and go look in the pickup. I am all out of beer. I won't drink anymore. You are more important to me than beer."

Not believing him, but wanting to encourage him to succeed, Flora had turned in his arms, and moved her face to avoid his breath. "Well, I hope you mean it. A week or two won't impress me. This needs to be quits for good." She'd heard her own calm tone, and wondered where this kind of calm was coming from—maybe it comes when one has quit caring.

What followed had been awful. Before nightfall, Henry was sweating and drinking up all the orange juice from the refrigerator. He didn't help her at all with the farm work, but instead went to bed. And he would have nothing to do with Patty. Of course, Patty was used to being without a father, and she'd long ago stopped asking if her dad would be at any of her music presentations at school.

And, for a couple days, Flora had seen such shaking and heard Henry doing so much retching in the bathroom that she'd begun to wonder if there could possibly be something dangerous about a drunk giving up his alcohol.

After some time passed, he had finally begun to feel well, and had begun to seem almost arrogant about his conquest. He began to mark X's on the calendar, showing her how long he'd been sober. He began to do better about taking care of the work in the fields, and was at home in time to milk the cows in the evening.

Flora had begun to hope that this might last, when after two weeks she had seen Henry actually showing interest in what Patty was learning at school. Patty had even asked her dad if he would be at her band night, as she was to play in an instrument trio. And Henry had promised to be there!

On the morning of Patty's musical, it seemed to Flora that Patty had dressed with more care than ever, and she'd mentioned her dad again when she was leaving to get on the school bus. And Flora would never forget the way, after the band members filed in and were seated, Patty's eyes gazed about the audience, searching for her parents. She had finally found where Flora sat, sitting too far from Patty for her to see her mother's unshed tears pooling in her eyes. Patty's face had looked like she must have made a mistake, and the eyes searched either side of where Flora sat. But, no empty chair was being held for Henry. Her dad was not there again. The quick hurt expression was replaced with a shut-down, defiant look. Patty's trio was magnificent. Perhaps she'd never played so well.

Henry's pickup wasn't home when Flora had driven in with a quiet Patty in the car. Patty had kissed her mother goodnight and disappeared into her room without a word.

Flora didn't say anything when Henry padded into the house in the wee hours of the morning. She lay quietly upon the sofa and no words were necessary.

Now, two days later, Henry was wanting her to accompany him on a "date" to the outdoor movies. She had no desire to go on a date with this man, but she did wonder what it would be like to go to the drive-in movies. She'd heard that some of the other farm families out here made the Fourth of July a special night and went to Riverton for the movies and the fireworks. The theater made it a family special for the holiday, and charged a dollar for a whole carload.

Flora stood and stepped closer to her husband, close enough to draw in a deep breath without making a big production of it. Hmmm, it didn't smell like Henry had been drinking today. Perhaps he was trying to learn from his mistake of the other night. After all, he had done so well for so many weeks.

"Okay. I'll drive up the road and stop at the Elwoods'. I'll ask if the older of their girls, Deirdre, can come over and watch Patty. What time would I say we would pick her up?"

Henry's face was beaming. He almost looked like a weathered, older version of the young soldier boy she had married in what seemed like centuries ago.

Flora crouched and pulled up a handful of small radishes. It was good to go with a gift when asking a favor. She didn't even know how much a babysitter should get paid these days.

She drove the 1959 Plymouth down the gravelly road, the dust pouring out behind, leaving her husband to finish the hoeing. That was a first!

What was she seeing up ahead? It looked like a young girl running in rapid strides down the dirt and gravel road. It was! That was Deirdre she was approaching.

Flora stopped the car a bit ahead of the girl and got out to stop her. "Where are you going in such a hurry? Is something wrong? Can I help?" Flora was worried as she heard the girl's breath coming in hiccupping sobs, and saw her holding her side. And the girl had no shoes on; blood was mixed with dust on the bottoms of her feet.

"Oh, Mrs. Zanders, the cows got into the alfalfa field and they all got bloated. They are dying in the corral. My mom has driven some into the stanchions and is pouring detergent down their throats. But, only four at a time fit in the stanchions, and it's too slow-going. Some need to be stuck with the trocar, but I'm not strong enough to drive it through the cow's hide, even though I can tell you how far from the hip bone one must stab it in. I have to get to Jack's house and see if he can come and help. Daddy's in Riverton at the dentist's."

"Get in; I'll drive you there." The passenger door had barely slammed shut when Flora's tires spun in the gravel. "Why didn't you phone Jack?" She thought to ask.

"Phones are out. Been out a couple days." Deirdre's face was drawn in adult-like worry. Flora wondered if she was afraid her parents would lose their livelihood, or if her kind heart was hurting over the suffering animals. Maybe both.

"Good thing you're a fast runner. Here we are."

Both hurried from the car, but Deirdre's long, running steps raced for the Browns' door. Her beating upon the door brought no one. Flora glanced around the yard. "Their car's not here! Get in, Deirdre. We'll drive home and get Henry. He's strong. He can drive those instruments into your cows."

Henry was still in the garden when Flora arrived. He looked confused when he saw Deirdre sitting in the car. "Not tonight, dear ..." he started to say as he approached the car.

"Henry, the Elwoods are having an emergency. Their cows are bloated and dying. They need us to help. Let Patty know we'll be gone awhile."

Henry dropped the hoe and raced to the house, yelling to Patty that they'd be back after a while. He leaped into the back seat, saying "Let's go."

"Back there. Drive back by the barn!" Deirdre directed Flora's parking.

As the three jumped from the vehicle, they could hear Charlotte calling out to Deirdre's sister, "She's going down! She's going down! There, Gloria, beat that cow, Suzy! Make Suzy get up. She'll die if we don't get her to her feet!"

"She won't get up, Mama!" Gloria's cry was nearing hysteria. "I can't make her get up!" The sound of a stick whacking loudly on the side of the cow was broken with the loud, drawn-out bellow of an animal in deathly pain.

Henry climbed the corral fence and dropped to the inner side of the cattle pen. He raced to where Gloria held a stick in one hand and a metal tool in the other.

Deirdre was right behind Henry. "Quick! She's holding the trocar." The older girl grabbed it from her younger sister's hand, and laid her own hand against the cow's hip, forming her hand in the shape of a backwards L. With the point of the instrument held in the space between her fore finger and her thumb, she gestured that this is where the trocar must be driven in.

She looked up at Henry's ashen face. "Dad pulls his arm back and spears it into the cow right here."

Henry had never seen such a nightmare.

The cow lay on her side, her legs stuck out in front of her and her head thrown back, seeming to gasp between those heart-wrenching bellows. Her side was blown up into an enormous size. The toxic air inside the cow was expanding rapidly and closing down her breathing and suffocating her.

"Get me a board or a hammer," he commanded as he held the trocar in place. The two girls ran in separate directions.

Flora had taken a look around the corral and seen the huge, blown-up cows standing uncomfortably, shifting from foot to foot. One cow was on the ground and obviously dead in the midst of them. Flora left Henry to deal with his cow, and hurried in to where she'd seen Charlotte ducking back into the barn.

She was amazed to see Charlotte standing in front of a stanchion, pushing a long length of garden hose down a cow's throat, and throwing small cups full of laundry detergent powder down the cow's mouth. Another cow next to her stood with its head in the stanchion and a hose coming from its mouth, with green froth pouring out.

"What shall I do?" She asked Charlotte.

"Get back here with me. Take over this job with this cow." Charlotte's answer was terse and she didn't glance in her neighbor's direction. Flora took hold of the cow's chin and began to throw more detergent in as Charlotte pushed past her.

Charlotte pulled the hose from the nearby frothing cow, opened the stanchion, and drove the cow out the barn door, hurrying to entice another cow into the open stanchion.

Flora's cow began to belch and blow out green froth from the tube, too.

"If the hose stops up, you'll need to pull it out and knock out the alfalfa chunks," Charlotte advised her with a quick look in her direction.

Now Mrs. Elwood had a tube and some more soap down the new cow's throat. She was moving back and forth between the two Holsteins, throwing more detergent into each one's mouth.

"I'm surprised the cows put up with this," Flora couldn't help saying.

"It feels like relief to the cows. They know they're about to die," Charlotte answered, between murmuring comforting words to the cows. She was calling each by name, Pansy, Gertrude, Heidi, Bossy, "We've got too many too badly bloated. We won't get through the herd fast enough at this rate. Dear Lord, please let John get home in time."

John saw Zanders' car in his yard as he arrived. This was a very unusual sight and he wondered if the Zanders were having trouble at their farm. He went to the house, but saw no one there, and realized he was hearing some ominous sounds from his cow yard.

"Damn. They got into the fresh-rained alfalfa," he breathed aloud as he raised his dress shoes to run towards his cows.

He was over the fence in one swift motion and found Henry beating the trocar into his best cow with a hammer. "Quick. There's one going down over there. Take the trocar over there and pound it into her. Deirdre, help him see where to spot the trocar on Julia." John pulled his pocketknife from his pocket and wiped it on his pants leg before he knelt over the cow that Jack had left. He pushed the blade into the hole made by the trocar where slight bubbling was coming too slowly. He gritted his teeth as he used his strength to pull the blade through the hide. He glanced up at his youngest daughter, tears staining her cheeks as she watched the suffering cows. "Gloria, get my big knife from where it hangs inside the barn door."

Gloria was back in a flash, so that John could substitute the large knife for his pocketknife, now cutting down into the cow's stomach. He reached inside and began to pull out the alfalfa that looked a bit like wet hay. Green froth and juice poured out over the cow's side and she began to let out more bellowing sounds. At least she was alive enough to do that.

Out of the corner of his vision, he could see his young daughter, Gloria, vomiting.

John looked towards where Zanders was kneeling over the cow Julie. It looked like she would need the knife, too. He pulled another wad from the belly of this cow, Prize, before he strode over to Julie. "I'll use my knife. See if your wife needs help." He beckoned his head towards the barn door where Flora was driving out a cow slinging green froth from her mouth.

As he bent over Julie, John looked back again at Prize. He could see she was moving more now, apparently her airways opening more. He might have saved her, if she didn't get infected from the non-sterile surgery.

He heard the bellows now coming from Julie, meaning time was slim. He thrust the knife into her side and began to pull the green wads of sinful dinner from her stomach, too. They would have to invest in some of that new medication that can be put into the cow's feed while milking. It was supposed to make the cows immune to bloat even if they jumped the fence and got into an alfalfa field they weren't supposed to. But, the vet had told him that some cows learn to eat around it. And that would be one more cost, too.

John was on his feet, moving to check Prize again, and glancing back at Julie who seemed to be breathing better, and was now actually trying to get on her feet again. He could see that his wife and Flora had sent out about twelve cows that had gained some relief from the detergent. He moved among his herd, some of whom were moaning and moving from foot to foot. He looked into the barn and saw that Flora and Charlotte had a good assembly line going there. Charlotte inserted the hose, and Flora moved along the four cows' mouths, throwing in the detergent. All four in the stanchions looked like they were going to survive.

Stepping back into the cow lot, he saw another looking like she was going to go down. He hurried to her side, positioned his hand by her hip bone, and thrust in the trocar. He pulled out the inner instrument, leaving the hollow sheath in her side to allow the froth to come out in a hiss.

He moved towards Sally and felt of her tight hide, spreading over her expanding side. She was showing great discomfort, too. He shoved the trocar into her side, jerking it out quickly, hoping the air could escape without the sheath of the trocar. He wished he had a second instrument. Who would ever have thought it could be necessary to have more than one trocar on hand?

Okay. Two more cows were being driven out of the barn by Henry. John chose the two that looked the most miserable in the cow yard, and drove them inside to place their heads in the stanchions. "We're making headway, Charlotte!" he said, attempting to brighten the stark look on his wife's face as he dashed back out to the cow lot.

Henry was jumping back over the fence and loping towards the car. "Gotta get more detergent," he yelled.

His car dug up part of their driveway, speeding out to the road.

Prize was still on her side, but she was breathing well. She probably was in shock and pain from the bloat and the surgery. She wouldn't like it much when he could get around to pouring some stinging Merthiolate on her.

Julie was on her feet, looking pretty miserable, but very alive. There were only two others that looked very serious now, and oh, good—there was Flora driving another one from the barn, so the stanchion was now clear for this one, Blackie. John slapped her flank and called her name authoritatively; Blackie swayed into the barn, too.

John retrieved the trocar sheath from the cow whose hide had loosened a bit by now, and pushed the other instrument inside it. He'd give the barn brigade a couple more minutes before thrusting the trocar into this last cow. Ah ... another empty in the stanchions. He drove another uncomfortable cow into the barn. He could see that those remaining in the cow lot had either not eaten so much of the alfalfa or had somehow digested it differently. Enough time had now elapsed since the dairy herd was discovered in the alfalfa field that the cows who were going to be in trouble had already become apparent.

Henry was back already with a big box of Flora's detergent. John could see it was a different kind than they usually used for this, but beggars couldn't be choosers. John stepped into the barn again, in time to see Flora and Henry working side by side, throwing soap down the cows' throats. Green froth had been slung onto Flora's pink polka dot blouse, and Henry had some green atop his bald spot amid his red hair. And Charlotte? Where was Charlotte? Oh, there, pushing a hose deep down inside the cow's stomach. Didn't she look beautiful, with her blond curls hanging over one eye!

John went to her and said, "Let me take it. Maybe you can bring all the Merthiolate you can find. We have some cows cut open in the corral. I don't know where the girls disappeared to. And what about Kevin?"

"He's spending the night with his friend from school." Charlotte's voice was exhausted, but her step was purposeful as she headed for the house to find something to pour onto the cows' wounds. Could it be possible that they had saved most of the herd? She knew that one was dead for sure. Only the Lord could have alerted her to go check on the cows in the middle of the day—it had been hours away from the time they usually drove them in for milking. But she'd suddenly known that she'd better make sure the cows had not broken down the fence to get into the alfalfa field after that nice summer rain. She silently thanked God over and over again as she strode to the house.

Finding the antiseptic medication, she hurried back to the corral. She prayed aloud now as she moved: "Dear Lord, You are so good to us. Thank you for helping us save our herd. Please help those ones that have been cut open to get well without too many complications. Thank you for sending the Zanders to help us, and for sending John home in time, too. You are so good, Lord. Amen."

She passed Deirdre holding Gloria in her arms against the corral fence. Gloria looked very pale. "We've about got it licked, Girls," Charlotte offered, giving a word of hope to her daughters without a break in her stride.

Handing the medicine to her husband, who was now flanked by Henry, she returned to the task of finishing driving the remaining cows from the stanchions. Flora's face was flushed and green slime streaked her face and her clothes. But when Charlotte took the push broom and began to sweep out the mess from the barn floor, Flora's face broke into a grin that soon turned into a merry laugh.

Charlotte looked at her and began to laugh, too, until she finally had to lean on the broom with tears running down her face.

Flora moved to Charlotte and put her hand on her neighbor's arm. "Wow, woman. You are quite a wonder when you are in motion!"

Still laughing, Charlotte placed the broom against the inner wall of the barn, and wrapped Flora in a hug. "How did you happen to end up here in the middle of this mess, anyway?"

While Flora explained how she'd been on the way to ask Deirdre to babysit in a few days, Henry returned to the barn. He moved to Flora's side. "What do you say? Can I possibly offer you a date more exciting than this one?"

Charlotte left them standing there, and joined John in the cow lot. She looked around and saw the wounded cattle, and noticed a couple cows nosing the dead cow near the fence. John stood up from pouring the antiseptic on Prize's gaping wound. Charlotte's eyes met his, seeing the relief registering there.

She murmured, "It looks a bit like there's been a war here."

"Well, then, this is one war we may have won." John's voice held awe. "You sure did well with taking things in hand the way you did." This was a compliment Charlotte would hug to her breast always. John wasn't given to offering compliments.

"I just wish they wouldn't have gotten out in the alfalfa. I thank God for nudging me to go check the cows at that time of day. Boy, those cows sure did seem angry that the girls and I were trying to drive them from the alfalfa field!"

"I'll check the fence to see where they pushed through before we release them from the corral. It'll be time to milk in an hour, but I doubt they'll be giving much milk tonight. We'll have to see if we can relieve Prize of some of her milk, but it'll be drying up soon after all this. I hope we can save her. She's going to be one sick cow with the rough surgery I performed on her. Let's see if we can lay a sheet over her to keep the flies out of her wound."

Henry and Flora approached the Elwoods as Gloria and Deirdre came to stand by their parents. Flora asked Deirdre if she would be willing to come stay with Patty while she and Henry went to the movies on Saturday night.

"Yes, glad to. You helped us save our cows," Deirdre answered promptly.

"I don't know how much you get for babysitting these days?" Flora asked.

"Well, other neighbors pay me one dollar each time I sit, and if it's more than three hours, they pay me two dollars."

"We can handle that," said Henry, grinning. "It's a date!"

CHAPTER 32

Mountains Beckon

"OH, SOPHIA, I should have also told them about the sheep stuck in the bog." Jack held his head in his hands as he sat upon their sofa. "I just don't know if the Senators can understand the desperate nature of our situation."

Sophia went to her husband and moved his hands so that she could see his eyes. "Look at me, Mr. Brown! You did your very best, and I was very proud to hear how honest you were as you told them about our farming life on Third Division. Anyone would be nervous talking in front of a Senate Committee! But no one would have guessed that you were the least bit nervous, listening to you talk to those high-falutin Senators."

"Most of us who testified were in favor of abolishing our homestead project here. I wonder if those Senators have any idea at all of what it's like to fight for our country, putting our very lives on the line, to come home safely and work very hard to raise our families, and then to realize that our own government had presented us with a contract that basically cheats us. We were required to prove that we were honest in meeting all the conditions they asked of us, but then the government didn't behave honestly in return. And now the government wants us to pay them back for all the drains they put on our land even though their fix doesn't work! In fact, not only that, but our sheep get stuck in them.

"And now the Bureau of Reclamation threatens to shut off our water if we don't agree to their plan! They're heartless, the whole lot of them! They must know we're lucky to make enough just to feed ourselves, while irrigating this land that doesn't seep out. Why, right now, only half of the land we own can be irrigated; the rest just lies there crusting up with alkali. So, just shut off the water and starve us out! How is that supposed to help us repay twenty million dollars?"

Their daughter Linda had entered the living room during her father's tirade, apparently wanting to ask for some kind of permission, but after a few minutes she'd just shaken her head and quietly left. There was no interrupting her parents when they were talking of repayment plans and Senate Hearings.

Sophia nodded reassuringly to Jack. "Dear, you did a good job in your speech at the Senate Hearing. You farmers have all been very smart to approach Senator Hickey and ask him to help. He's been sympathetic to this homestead project for years."

She took Jack's hand and tugged him to his feet. "Come on, Honey, let's get some neighbors together and drive up to the mountains for a day of picnicking and trout fishing. We all need to get our minds off all this worry, and enjoy some of the benefits of living in Wyoming. We're having magnificent weather!"

Jack accompanied Sophia to the front door and the two stepped out onto their front porch. The weather was unseasonably warm—one of those rare times that occurred in early winter, called Indian summer. Yes, it would be perfect, tomorrow after church, to go to the mountains for a day of fun.

"Okay, Sophia, you win. Call John and Charlotte and see if their family would like to ride up in our truck. We might also call and include Henry and Flora with their daughter." For this sort of outing, Sophia would take all the benches and chairs from their kitchen and place them in the back of their big truck. She would include quilts to cover their legs as they rode up to the mountain range. They would reach about 5,500 feet in altitude. The air would be thinner and chillier up there, and they would see snow melting in places along the road.

As Sophia made the telephone calls, Jack began to rummage around in the closet. He dug out the ragbag, finding the red flannel from Sophia's worn-out nightgown, and sat down to make some new fly hooks for fishing. He deftly wrapped the colorful feathers about the flannel.

The farmers had been forewarned that more hearings would be necessary, perhaps even in Washington. It was painful to have to think about letting this land go, along with all the dreams he and Sophia had held when they arrived.

And he had to admit, it would be about as hard to leave his neighbor, John, as the land itself. John and he had shared a lot. They rarely talked of their military memories, except for their common recurring bouts of the malady that John called his "old malaria." But, they held a mutual respect for the unspoken horrors of war that each had experienced. They understood being survivors after their time in Japan.

And he and John still took turns buying new farm implements, in spite of the FHA's efforts to have them each buy too many new pieces of equipment, calling it "capital investment." How on earth did the other farmers make it, those who had given in and bought so many new implements?

Winter would hit in full force soon, and they would be getting their annual Christmas card from the families who had left their Wyoming farms, after the 1953 Bill that had allowed him to nearly double his farm's size. He wondered if Jim, who had ended up in Arizona, was enjoying the persistent heat that he would experience on the Gila Project. Jack wondered how they irrigated down in Arizona. Jim's letters never did say. But, he did say they got more cuttings of hay.

"Both families are on!" Sophia stuck her head into the living room. "I had to wait quite a while to get to use the phone, as someone was on the party line every time I lifted the phone there for a bit."

"Flora is going to wring a couple of chicken's necks and fry them up for the picnic, and Charlotte says both the girls will join them on the outing. She's making some of that sand-cherry cobbler we all like so much. It will take more seating than we used to manage when the children were all so little."

Jack imagined that the children would be doing a lot of things differently compared to when they were little. It seemed his own children's noses were stuck in a book most of the time these days. No more grabbing a stick and riding it around whimsically, pretending it was a horse.

He thought of Georgie, getting ready to use his slide rule in math now. Perhaps George (as he now insisted on being called) would think the outing was only for those less mature than himself and would refuse to go. It was getting harder and harder to find activities that everyone wanted to join in. Man, it used to be fun when they would go for a day of "rock hunting" and sometimes find arrowheads and other Indian artifacts, and also the buffalo horns they occasionally collected. But the children seemed to be each in their own worlds now.

Sophia was thinking of the children, too. She was aware that the kids were getting tired of all the fretful and fervent conversations about the Bureau of Reclamation, prices of water, and lately, Senate Hearings.

Sophia knew that Jack and John were now agreed in their thinking that their farms were not sufficient to provide a real living, and that there had to be a way to leave behind the farmland and without owing the huge debt the government was attempting to hang on them. She'd heard that some of the other homesteaders were determined to stay, no matter what. Jack and John seemed to have moved past that thinking, after trying to eek out a living for more than eleven years now.

Since all the farmers didn't seem to be of the same sentiment, there was beginning to be some tension at times when some of the farm families ran into each other. Charlotte had heard nothing of it yet from her children, but she wondered if the tension would reach the school kids. It would be a sad thing, indeed, if the children who had been as close as blood relatives would begin to distance themselves from each other. Why, they had as much as filled the place of "relatives" at each other's Christmases and Thanksgivings, since hardly any of the settlers had real relatives living nearby.

"Rachel, Linda!" Sophia called out the door for her daughters. They appeared to be enjoying the good weather by playing with the bum lamb in the yard. She watched young Rachel reach and hug the lamb's neck while Linda set the chicken-wire fence around the animal. Earpy wouldn't try to get out of the temporary pasture.

"What were you wanting, Linda?" Sophia hadn't forgotten her daughter's efforts to interrupt her father's flood of words.

Rachel grinned and winked and jabbed Linda in the ribs as her big sister's face grew pink and she swallowed hard.

Linda began, "Well, Robert asked me to go to the homecoming dance with him in two weeks. I'm not sure what I'd wear, but I would like to go."

Sophia drew in her breath. This was the era she'd been anticipating and dreading. She wasn't sure there were any local boys good enough for her girls.

Her voice was calm and low, "So, what do you like about Robert?"

"He's cute, and he wears his hair all waxed up in a point!" Rachel jeered, ducking the swing of Linda's arm.

"Now, Rachel, if you are to be here for this conversation, you are going to have to be quiet and respectful." Sophia couldn't help but smile at Rachel and give her a tiny wink.

"So what is your answer?" She turned to her oldest daughter, who was chewing on her lip.

"Robert is a very good dancer. I've seen him at some of the school dances.   He never has a date and asks all kinds of different girls to dance, so I think he is kind. He's asked me to dance a couple of times, and I was able to keep up with him pretty well. It would be fun to dance with him the whole evening. But, he's always honest; he'll say just what he thinks if one asks him. He's not phony like some of the boys that are always flirting with all the girls. And he pays attention in school and shows the teachers respect …" Linda had lifted an eyebrow and, with a growing smile, was searching her mother's face to see if she'd answered in the right manner yet.

"Well, I'll talk to your dad about it; you can have your answer for Robert on Monday." Sophia patted her daughter's shoulder. "We're going up to the mountains tomorrow after church. We'll take the truck up there, filling the back with the Zanders and the Elwoods. We will take advantage of one of these rare Indian summer days. Doesn't it sound fun?"

While Rachel seemed more excited about the family fun than Linda did, both were cooperative with the plan and began to discuss what they might take along to make it fun for everyone. They wondered if their dad could really get through a whole day without worrying aloud about this irrigation project.

CHAPTER 33

This Side of the Battle

"JOHN, WE MADE the Riverton Ranger again today." Newspaper articles regarding Third Division were becoming a regular thing in the local newspaper. Even though people living around Pavillion didn't get the paper until a day late, it was still interesting to see the reporters' views of the Third Division homesteaders. "This article is dated Monday, August 5, 1963. It says here that Senator Gale McGee is introducing a new bill this week wherein 'the Bureau of Reclamation will provide $11.9 million for rehabilitation for parts of the Third Division.'"

"Rehabilitation!?" John snorted. "It'll take more than rehabilitation to make this seeping land produce. Does it say anything about buying us out?"

Charlotte's eyes roved down the column. "Hmmm … water would be delivered for 10 years with settlers paying only the O & M charges for the 10-year period … A new 50-year repayment contract would be negotiated with Midvale Irrigation District …"

John was shifting impatiently. "None of that matters if McGee's Bill doesn't have a buy-out clause."

"Oh, here it is. Provision number 5: The Secretary of the Interior would be authorized to purchase existing farms at fair market value."

John was doing his well-practiced pacing. "And just what does 'fair market value' mean? That is going to be the telling part." He stopped and stared intently at Charlotte.

Charlotte's voice grew more cheerful. "John, John. Listen to this: 'McGee explained that "fair market value" will mean the value of the land as represented at the time of purchase, if the land has depreciated in value, or at present appreciated value.'" She lowered the paper and grinned triumphantly at John.

"That's it! Charlotte, that's it. That's what Senator Hickey has been fighting for!" John rushed to Charlotte's side and took the paper to see where her finger was pointing.

As he lowered his head over the news article, Charlotte could see the gray hair that was scattered through his sideburns now. His weathered complexion held permanent crow's feet and ruts along either side of his mouth. This climate had been hard on him; perhaps the worry had been harder. Both he and Charlotte were still lean, possibly because there was never an extra portion of anything she could find to put on the table.

The kids' growth didn't seem to be slowed with the lean meals; Kevin had headed off to college and Deirdre would be a senior next year. Even Gloria was in high school now. Maybe they'd get moved before half their kids had settled down here or else had taken off for different parts of the country. Charlotte would sure like to see her family remain as intact as possible when they resettled somewhere else.

"I must go see Jack. He doesn't take the paper. Unless he heard it on the radio or saw it on the television news, he won't know for sure about this latest Bill. Thank the Lord, it appears to match the letter we got from the Department of the Interior, Bureau of Reclamation last March. This has been a long journey, with three Senate Committee meetings and one House Hearing, too, to this point."

John appeared absent-minded as he tied the canvas hay apron across the legs of his blue jeans and pushed on his felt Western hat. The door shut behind him with a snap.

Charlotte began to pick up the lunch dishes and place them in the sink. If the Bill was introduced in Congress this session, they could actually see an end to their predicament in the next year or so. Unless, of course, the Bill stalled out …

Boy, she wished they didn't have a party line. She would love to just pick up the telephone and call her mother and try to help them understand back in Kansas.

Mama had looked aghast when she'd told her that the Third Division farmers were going to join together to sue the government. Charlotte doubted that any of the good folks out here on the homestead had ever thought they'd be involved in litigation, but the misrepresentation of the land had to be righted.

John's truck needed brakes again. His brakes were squealing and grinding as he pulled to a stop beside Jack's hayfield. Jack was getting his hay in by himself. Usually they helped each other with putting the hay on the wagon to haul it to the haystacks, but this morning John had been in town, getting more binding twine for the baling he would start tomorrow.

John climbed the fence and strode to the side of Jack's hay wagon. He liked his homemade "slip" better because when his tractor pulled the wooden sheet across the hay stubble, one didn't have to lift the heavy bale so high as one did to get it up into this wagon. But Jack liked the tall sides, and it did carry more hay at one time if there was an extra fellow in the wagon to help maneuver the bales up to a third row or more.

Jack had seen John approaching and left the wagon to go get back on the tractor. Jack was quite worn out by now, from jumping up and down off that tractor and doing all the lifting of the bales, too. He was glad to drive for a while and let John walk along to pick up the bales for the wagon.

Bale after bale, John heaved up the rectangular bale by the twine and balanced it against his hay-apron-clad knee to boost the bale onto the wagon. Finally, he gestured to Jack that the wagon held all the bales he could toss onto it. Jack stopped the tractor while John climbed onto the back and held on.

Then, Jack moved the tractor into high gear and the loud sound of the tractor's putt-putt cut through the August air. When the haystack was reached, John jumped to the ground and began to remove the bales from the wagon. Jack crawled up on the existing rows of hay and pulled the bales higher onto the stack as John placed them near Jack's feet.

The men worked in a comfortable silence; after thirteen years of partnership it was easy to settle into a steady, practiced rhythm. When the wagon was unloaded, John pulled a hay stem from a nearby bale, stuck it in his mouth, and sat down on the lowest row of the haystack. Jack recognized the cue for a break, and brought the two canteens from the tractor, handing one to his friend.

Seating himself alongside John, he took a long drink of the water. Jack's water was good well water. It should be; John had witched that well, like he had eight or nine others on this homestead.

John removed his hay stem and took a drink also, wiping his mouth on his dusty sleeve. His face came up smudged. "I brought you something." He reached in his back pocket and brought out the article Charlotte had read to him. He was silent as Jack read the piece to himself.

Jack's eyes were bright when he raised them from the paper. "Well. This is sounding more like it might turn out alright."

"It's about time that our situation here was taken seriously." John turned his body so that he could peer more comfortably at his neighbor. "Good thing the twenty-one of us were willing to file suit against the federal government. Lord knows, I've never really believed in lawsuits, thinking most who filed them were just out to get something for nothing. But, with the help of former Senator Joe Hickey, I think we might have helped the government realize, at last, that this has to go beyond talk, talk, talk."

"Have you thought about what you would do if you were to move from your farm here, John?" Jack was standing again, looking back at his hayfield, torn between hopes of the future and the demands of today.

"You could bet I wouldn't be settling down on a piece of land that requires irrigation. Although chances are good we'd not find another piece of ground anywhere that would again hold this formula of 'heavy clay underlain by sandstone and shallow decomposed shale,' as they now call it. That's what they say makes the soil waterlogged with 'high amounts of alkali.'"

"All I know is that the alkali area doesn't grow anything. It's hard for me to think beyond the battle, John. We've battled snakes and aphids and coyotes. Now we've been battling the bureaucrats, too. Right now, though, I think we'd better carry on the battle of getting in all our hay before it rains. Ready?" Jack was heading back to his tractor, his canteen strap slung over his shoulder. "This time, you drive the tractor and I'll pick up the bales."

John sighed and rose quickly to his feet. Jack had a point. It was hard to imagine being on the other side of the battle.

CHAPTER 34

New Tensions

"MOM, SOME OF my friends are acting downright hostile now." Gloria sat on the kitchen table, swinging one leg across her other knee. She had been trying to explain to Charlotte how her school life had changed.

Charlotte turned from where she was whipping some thick cream for supper. She carefully set the eggbeater down in the bowl and wiped her hands on her apron. She stepped toward Gloria.

"Why do you think the friends are acting differently now?"

Gloria scooted off the table and pulled the fly-swatter from the hook on the counter. She gave a wide swing at a buzzing fly. "It's about this 'Third Division' stuff. Harry says now his family is going to have to move away, and he'll have to leave the basketball team he's been doing so well on. And Shirley says it's our own fault; that we never knew how to farm ..."

Her mother put an arm about Gloria's shoulder and took the fly-swatter from her. She deftly reached out and smacked the fly to its death. With another swift movement, she had its remains balanced on the swatter. "Honey, everyone grieves differently. I hear that anger is one stage of grief. Some of those families may not have stayed so involved in the battle over this land as our family did. You can't blame them. They were probably so busy trying to make their farms bring in a living that they were just putting one foot in front of the other. Now, they find it's time to figure out a real solution, and it may be a bit of a shock."

"I suppose," said Gloria, pulling up her bobby socks and patting them into place. "But I miss the way things were. We all seemed like such good friends, and now there's all this tension. Good Heavens! We were all in 4-H together for years!"

"Well, Darling, remember to treat them the nice way you always have. Some day soon, you'll live in a different place. You won't want to give them reason to think any worse of you than they are determined to do. I believe they'll soon have to begin to embrace ideas of their own new lives, too, and they'll forget their animosity towards each other." Charlotte hoped her words made sense to her daughter. She wasn't sure they made too much sense to her own ears.

She moved back to the whipping cream, not wanting to lose the chance for it to develop into stiff peaks. Picking up the beater, she began to rapidly turn the handle, careful to keep the beater tilted so the cream didn't fly out of the bowl.

The telephone rang for their family, two longs and a short ring.

Gloria ran to answer the phone, calling, "I hope it's Ronny!"

Charlotte smiled. Although Ronny lived in Torrington and they didn't see each other often, Gloria and the boy seemed to enjoy each other a lot.

"Ronny. I was hoping it was you." Gloria's voice was dropping now and she walked so that the coiled telephone line was stretched taut before she flopped down in a chair with her feet stretched out in front of her. The call wouldn't be long; this was a long-distance call for her boyfriend.

Charlotte was already deep in her own thoughts. She was recalling the difficult conversation she'd had with Sophia yesterday. Sophia had been telling her that she and Jack had about settled upon the plan of moving to Utah, where Jack's family had some land. Their reaching a decision was making this idea of leaving more real for Charlotte. She wasn't going to be sad to leave behind the financial woes that went with this bog land. But she had enjoyed this house that her husband had built them, allowing her to raise her children with a real bathroom and a refrigerator, too. And now, in the last few years, a telephone and even a television! The years of the outhouse seemed a long way back. But, actually, it had just been twelve years since they moved into their "new" house, leaving behind the "chicken house."

She and John had been subscribing to farm-sale catalogues for the past six months. They had discovered that the children were better able to adjust to changes if they allowed the kids to be in on the dreaming, too. The girls would pore over the catalogues for hours, imagining out loud what it might be like to live in a house with an upstairs, or how it might be exciting to live closer to a big city. Their closest town had always been Pavillion, which was lucky to host 200 people. None of the farm families had ever even bothered to learn if there were street names; the place was so tiny, everyone knew the way to anywhere they needed to go.

Charlotte could see that the girls were beginning to be excited about the adventure of a move. While they each had a boy they were fond of, they could be overheard thinking it could be fun to be the "new kid" in school, with a chance to arrive without the baggage of being remembered all the way back to the awkward first grade. Charlotte figured that she and John would be able to pry the girls away from their boyfriends without too much trouble.

And, how could she imagine life without her special friend, Sophia? John was also such a good friend with Jack. It would be hard to imagine a life without that couple being a part of it.

She had been John's partner in working this land. Yes, she liked this house, but her devotion was to her husband

and her family. She knew John was devoted to her and the family, too, but she'd also witnessed him experience true love for his land. She'd watched him tromp miles, day after day, to irrigate the land, killing snakes along the way, as he trusted his beloved land to produce for his family. She'd been alongside him as he gazed warmly upon the height his trees had reached in the windbreak he'd planted so tediously, with Kevin's help when Kevin was still small.

She and Sophia had talked about their men's attachment to the land, and wondered how their husbands would really do when it came time to uproot them from it. They had searched for words to describe the betrayal of the land, and it was Sophia who had said it was "a bit like a treacherous seductress."

Charlotte sprinkled sugar into her heavy cream and beat it slowly a couple minutes longer, insuring stiff peaks in her whipped cream. She covered the bowl with a dish towel and slid it into the refrigerator. It would be a nice addition to the butterscotch pudding she had cooked a bit earlier.

She pulled off her apron and laid it across the back of a kitchen chair, and moved into the service porch. There, she pulled down the bandanna and pushed it against her nose. Phew! Good thing tomorrow was washday; the scarf was strong with the pungent smell of the cow barn. Even though it was smelly, she tied it over her head, having found that the plaid scrap could prevent flecks of cow manure from landing in her hair when a cow switched its tail. She'd better get the milking started.

John would be in from the field soon to join her. It would take them two hours to milk the forty cows.

Good! A glance at the telephone told her that Gloria had hung up the telephone receiver some time ago, and had gotten out her homework.

CHAPTER 35

The 'Option'

FLORA ROSE FROM her familiar bed on the living-room couch. She folded the blankets, stacked them beside the couch, and covered the pile with the embroidered dresser scarf. That way, if company should come, it wouldn't be so obvious about the rift in her marriage.

She had the couch cushions fluffed up and looking normal before Patty showed up for breakfast.

"Mom, the kids at school are talking about where they are moving, now that the U.S. Government has agreed to buy us out. What are we going to do?"

"Sweetheart, we've not come to a conclusion. Your dad seems to think we need to stay here and make the best of this situation."

"What about you, Mom? What would you like to do?"

A novel idea! Her opinion should count in this household, but it had been a long time since she'd heard anything other than orders and demands from her husband. Why, the last good time they'd truly enjoyed together had been that time Henry had taken her to the drive-in movies for their anniversary. They had watched such an odd show, "The Creature Walks Among Us." She still shivered whenever she remembered some of the scenes in it. After Henry had driven their babysitter Deirdre home, he'd made sweet love to her, all full of dreams for their future. That night she'd forgotten for a moment her fear that he might have gotten syphilis from some wild woman during his drunken nights out prowling.

Shaking her black head of hair, now streaked with white, Flora gave a faint smile and answered her daughter's question. "Well, I think it might be nice to live in a town again. I've worked this land about as much as I think I want to."

Patty reached down from her height–very tall for a girl, at five feet nine inches–and hugged her mom, who felt lean, with tight muscles. "Me, too, Mom. I'm ready for a real change. Maybe I should try to work on Dad."

Flora's brows pulled low. "No, I don't think so. He isn't in an agreeable mood much these days. We'd best hope that some of the other farmers will run into him and have a sensible talk with him." But Flora knew it was unlikely that any of the other homesteaders would be encountering Henry. He didn't mingle much with the other men out here, the ones who worked so hard.

Their paths didn't cross. He was up by noon, off to the fields for a bit, and then off to the bar, she presumed. She never went looking for him. It would be too shaming to be seen driving by the bar, hoping for a glimpse of her husband's pickup.

The fields were not producing much. Flora found she didn't have the heart to do much irrigating these days; she found herself too resentful of the trap Henry had brought her to. It might be different if he were ill with polio or some other dread disease, and she could see that he couldn't help it.

But, within a day of having taken her to the picture show, he had come back home drunk as ever. The three years since then had been tedious, watching her husband's steady decline. He lied more than ever, and even resorted to taking money from her purse. He had staggered and fallen drunkenly against that kettle of boiling water, and gotten those burns clear down his legs.

And the things he called her! She'd had to go to the dictionary to later look up some of those names, never having heard such dirty words. She was happy to allow Patty to spend the night more and more with her special friend Sally, from her class at school. It wasn't lost upon her that Patty never asked to have Sally stay the night at their house.

She set the corn flakes and milk on the table and wished her daughter a good day as she headed to the barn to milk their remaining cow. She had traded the other cow, to the dismay of Henry, for a couple pigs. It was going to be nice to have some bacon again one of these days! She couldn't see that they needed milk from two cows. Besides, the last time she had worked so hard to drive the cow up the ramp to the truck so she could haul her to the neighbor's bull, that cow hadn't even gotten with calf.

She had heard that some of the farmers were using a new technique called "artificial insemination" instead of bulls now, but it would be too humiliating to call and ask the veterinarian about such things—anyone could listen in on her call, what with their party line, after all, and they'd realize that she was the one really running this farm. At least when she drove the cows to meet with the bull, she could use the excuse that Henry was sick for the day.

She had just stood up from the milk stool where she'd squatted to milk the cow when Flora heard the roar of the school bus picking up speed, and knew that Patty had gotten onto the bus. She was a good girl, and certainly deserved a happier home than the one Flora had been able to provide.

She wished it were easier to get through to Henry. They didn't have long now to turn in their official choice of options. She had tried hard to stay up on this lawsuit business with their Third Division. She had read enough to know that each farm family had to meet the deadline for submitting their decision on whether they would opt to stay on their land or accept the U.S. Government's buy-out.

True, Henry saw no good from leaving their farm and would hear no argument, but Flora could see reality.

As she carried the milk bucket to the house, she was careful to not have the bubbles spill over the sides. She gazed about, trying to see what an appraiser would see if looking over their farm. There was the barn behind her, with the paint peeled off and the boards beginning to weather. The shingles on the log house were worn out, and there was a piece of tarp over the pitch of the roof where she'd recently crawled up there to try to stop a leak.

The porch of the house was sagging. She had propped it up with cinder blocks that she'd dragged home from Riverton, but her carpentry skills were minimal. When she'd tried to suggest to Henry that he might fix some of these things, he'd railed at her and called her an "ingrate."

Well, maybe he'd surprise her and be up already when she entered the house. Making sure she wasn't quiet about it, she let the screen door slam behind her, and pulled the inner door shut with a bang.

No sign of anyone having been in the kitchen. The dishes from Patty's breakfast were neatly stacked in the sink where Patty would have put them. The sun shone brightly through the kitchen window, showing off the African violets that were blooming on the windowsill.

Using a filter, Flora poured the milk from the bucket into a gallon jar that stood in the sink. The cow was doing well, giving so much milk!

Flora wondered what mood Henry would be in today; his mood served as the barometer of what type of day she would have. She spent a lot of her time in a tentative space, feeling almost like she was holding her breath. It was a pity when a woman liked the part of her day best after her husband had thrown a fit and driven away!

What was that sound? Flora froze where she stood. Every sense was heightened as she cocked an ear towards the master bedroom. It sounded like things breaking. Was that the lamp? What on earth could he be so angry about this early in the morning?

Flora tip-toed to the bedroom door, opened the door quietly, and peeped inside, ready to duck.

What in the world? Fear of Henry abruptly changed into fear for Henry. His body was thrashing about on the bed. Apparently, his out-flung arm had knocked the lamp off the stand onto the hardwood floor.

Moving quickly to his side, she leaned to unplug the lamp with one hand, while she laid the other hand on his convulsing body. "Henry, Henry! What is wrong?"

His eyes were rolled back and he was making a growling noise low in his throat.

Was this one of those seizures? Had he developed epilepsy? What was it that one is supposed to do for a seizure?

Flora could see his teeth were forced tightly shut, and blood trickled from his chin.

Dear God, what should I do? Flora thought of the telephone. She must call for help. She took off running for the phone. When she reached the kitchen, she was too worried to be polite as she told the neighbor already using the phone, "You must hang up. I have a medical emergency!" She heard someone say, "Oh!" followed by a quick click on the line.

She looked at the bulletin board hanging above the phone and located the number of their family doctor in Riverton. It would be a long-distance call. Oh, well! She began to talk as soon as the lady answered at the other end.

"I must know what to do. I think my husband is having a seizure. He's jerking all over the bed. What? Oh, yes, of course; please get the doctor for me ... Yes, well ..." Stretching the phone line as far as she could, she peered down the hall into the open bedroom door. Every muscle in Henry's body was still moving in that jerking motion.

"Hello. This is Doctor Lawrence. Who is this? What's happening there?"

Charlotte found she was crying. She sobbed, "Doctor. Thank God. This is Flora Zanders. My family comes to see you from our farm out here near Pavillion. You sewed up Henry's head last April after he got drunk and fell down those stairs ... It's Henry again. He's in bed and he seems to be seizuring or something. He won't stop jerking. His eyes are all rolled back, he's growling, and his mouth is bleeding ..."

The doctor's voice spoke over hers with welcome authority: "Mrs. Zanders, Mrs. Zanders, how long has he been seizing?"

Flora looked at the clock. She couldn't think. How long had it been? She'd heard the lamp hit the floor before she'd found him in this condition. Was the lamp at the start of this, or had it gone on longer?

"I'm not sure. I was outside and I just found him. It's been going on for ten minutes or more that I've seen now ... Oh, Doctor, what should I do?"

"Mrs. Zanders, ten minutes is a very long time for a seizure. I hope you are wrong. See if you can turn him on his side. It'll be too late to shove something into his mouth. He's probably bitten his tongue. On his side, he'll have less chance of swallowing it. And, Ma'am, when he stops the jerking, see if you can load him into the car and bring him into our office here in Riverton. We close at five o'clock."

"Yes, yes, thank you, Doctor." Flora had to hang up the telephone twice, missing the cradle with the receiver the first time she rammed it down.

Flora prayed under her breath as she turned back to the bedroom. *Lord help me.* Something had changed. The growling had stopped. Henry was quiet. Good! Maybe he had gotten over the seizure condition before she even rolled him onto his side.

"Henry?" He wasn't answering. His face was very purple, the blood staining his chin. She might as well roll him on his side, since that was all the doctor had told her for sure.

"Henry, Henry, the doctor says I should take you to town." Flora didn't know what was supposed to happen when the jerking stopped, but it would be very hard to load a man this big into the car when he wasn't moving at all. It looked to her like her husband's purple face was paling.

"Henry, are you even breathing?" Flora felt a chill. She put her cheek to his nose, and felt no breath at all. Where was one supposed to feel for a pulse? She yanked his shirt up and laid her head upon his chest. There was no sound, no movement. Her cheek against the red hair on his chest, she gazed towards his feet and saw that he had wet himself. From the smell of it, he'd done more than that.

Flora ran to the phone and called John Elwood. He would know. He'd seen plenty of dead varmints on his farm. Thank goodness, Charlotte answered right away, and said he was nearby and would be right over.

Flora bundled up the whiskey bottles from Henry's bedroom and threw them in the trash outdoors. No point in that being part of the gossip that was sure to go around after this.

If Henry wasn't dead, he was going to wish he were! And if he was, then she would be finding that "option" and sending it back today! She and Patty would be leaving this wretched piece of ground together.

CHAPTER 36

"**I** HEAR THERE'S a beautiful lake nearby where you'll be living." Jack grinned at John. "I guess you'll be fishing, with all that free time you'll have since you won't be stomping around in your hip-boots anymore."

John pulled his coat collar closer around his neck and pushed his gray felt hat down on his head, as though that would make him feel warmer. "Yep," he chuckled, "I will be fishing, and driving on asphalt roads to town, too!

"Actually," John continued, "the soil is so rich it is practically black. And the farm is two generations old; so any problems that were going to occur would have shown up by now. Pretty different from this old alkali seep land."

John turned and carefully leaned an elbow in between the barbs on the top wire of the fence. The countryside had an uncanny quiet to it. No tractors could be heard.

He gazed silently across his farmland. Well, for now it was still his farmland. He looked towards the house and all the outbuildings he had constructed on the home site. Charlotte would be busy tucking the last things into the car. The equipment had already been shipped out on a railroad flat car.

"Out of more than 300 acres, only 150 acres irrigatable! Boy, Jack, it sure did look promising back when we were clearing it, didn't it?"

Jack tightened his own earmuffs and slapped his gloved hands together. He blew his breath out in a cloud in front of him in the cold air. "Yes, and we've had some good times here, too, my friend. Remember when you came home and found the coyote had made its way into your little one-room cabin?"

John threw back his head in laughter. "Boy, Charlotte sure was unhappy about the blood on the floor when I shot him right then and there! Good thing she and the kids were gone. She's always said it was my fault the coyote got into the house; says I must've left the door open."

John's laughter came to an abrupt end, and he sighed deeply, eyes taking in the land again, with the purple mountains on the distant horizon. "You know, Jack, I am looking forward to my new farm, but it hurts like heck to have to leave this all behind. This old dirt truly holds our blood, sweat, and tears! I just never thought it would turn out this way."

Jack closed the space between the two, and laid his gloved hand on John's shoulder. "We did our best, partner. Better than our best. This land just wasn't tamable."

Jack gave his neighbor's shoulder another pat before sticking his hand in his own coat pocket. "Jeez, it's cold out here. Can't say I'm going to miss forty below zero too much. Must be about eight degrees right now, wouldn't you say?"

"Well, however cold it is, that dratted radio announcer is sure to say, "It's a beautiful day in Fremont County."

The two laughed in unison.

"How can a guy still love something so much that has done him so poorly?" John pondered aloud, sharing those innermost thoughts that were hard for him to expose to another fellow.

"Well, John," Jack seemed to drawl in his serious answer, "I've about figured it this way: This is the way it feels to have a divorce. We are forced to divorce a land that we still love. We can't have the beautiful traits of her without accepting all the dirty tricks she'll do us, too!"

John nodded, and turned to face his friend. "You are right, Jack. I am divorcing this Third Division land. It'll take a while to get over, but we'll heal, won't we?"

"Yes. If we've proven anything, it is what survivors we are. Why, this homesteading started out with eighty-seven of us. And a whole lot of the homesteaders had left their farms before this last Bill was passed to buy us out. But look at us now. There are just nine of us left from North Pavillion, and fifteen in the North Portal region. Twenty-four, out of eighty-seven homesteads;

that speaks pretty highly of our hard work and survival skills." Jack squared his shoulders.

It wasn't hard for John to imagine Jack as the former Army Sergeant, ready to snap a salute. John stomped his feet to attempt to warm them inside his boots. "I've heard of some men getting bitter after a divorce. They turn against all women afterwards. I guess if we are divorcing this Wyoming land, if we were truly bitter, we'd leave all farming behind ..."

"Well, then, bitter we aren't. Just a bit heartbroken, you might say." Jack's smile looked a bit forced. "We'd better get back to our women. They said their good-byes yesterday, and they'll be eager to get on the road."

John gazed back at his property with one last longing look. "Promise me you'll come out and see us sometime soon." He turned to look at his friend who was shaking his head.

"Nope. You know me well enough to know I don't make promises I don't keep. I reckon the women will write to each other, and we can keep in touch that way. It'll be a few years before we get things set up well enough to plan any big trips."

"Yes, you're probably right." John felt another stab of grief. His friend Jack was so much a part of this land to him. "Well, then, so long for now." He held out his hand and gave this sun-tanned and shivering man a hearty handshake and turned on his heel to get into his pickup.

Finding Charlotte at home, wiping down the linoleum kitchen floor, he was so glad that it wasn't her he was divorcing. This homestead land had brought many trials, but it had only brought the two of them closer. Not all of the couples on this treacherous land had fared so well.

Outside, he took another look around the buildings and saw that everything had been packed that they planned to take. There was nothing more to do here. So he returned to the house, and called the dog and put her in the truck cab with him. Charlotte would drive ahead with the girls and the cat. Whew! He was glad he'd be in this vehicle when that cat used the litter box!

There! The girls were carrying the cat out in her cage now. They looked as excited as though they were off on a vacation! Charlotte followed, locking the door one more time.

He gave Charlotte a kiss before she got into the car. "Hon, we are going on to a better place. But, we did our best here!" She blinked back a tear and slid into the car as he moved to the truck.

He drove far enough behind Charlotte so that the dirt road didn't blot his view with the dust storm the car threw up.

But, what was she doing up there in the road? It looked like his wife had stopped the car and backed it up, and then driven forward, only to stop suddenly. Surely they wouldn't be having car trouble already!

He stepped on the gas and caught up to her, driving alongside and rolling down the window. "What's going on?"

Charlotte flashed a broad smile as she rotated her arm, rolling down the window. John could hear his teen-aged girls laughing loudly from within the car.

"I just thought I should run over one more snake for good measure!" Charlotte called.

"Snakes? They're hibernating."

Charlotte laughed again, "Could've fooled me!" and threw the car into gear.

HISTORIC DOCUMENTS CONSULTED

Public Law 258, 83ʳᵈ Congress, Chapter 428, 1ˢᵗ Session, S. 887. 1953. Act approved August 13, 1953.

Commission on Organization of the Government. June 1955. *Findings of the Task Force on Water Resources and Power, Vol. 2*, pp. 1–12.

Third Division District Board of Commissioners. 1961. Letter to Mr. Bruce Johnson, Regional Director, U.S. Department of Interior, Bureau of Reclamation, May 5, pp. 1–3.

Subcommittee on Irrigation and Reclamation, and Committee on Interior and Insular Affairs, United States

Senate, 87th Congress, 1st session. 1961. Hearings on the Third Division Irrigation District of the Riverton Project, Riverton, Wyoming, October 31, pp. 1–4.

"Farmers … Can Afford Nothing," *Riverton (Wyo) RANGER*, May 16, 1961, p. 7.

"24 Farmers Stay, 3rd Division," *Riverton (Wyo) RANGER*, May 18, 1961.

Talbott, Allen D. 1961. Secretary-Treasurer of Commissioners, Third Division Irrigation District. Letter to the Senate Subcommittee on Irrigation and Reclamation, United States Senate. October 31, 1961, pp. 1–3.

"New Bill on Local Project Both 3rd Division, Midvale," *Riverton (Wyo) RANGER*, August 5, 1963, p. 16.

"The Riverton Reclamation Study Report Released Today," *Riverton (Wyo) RANGER*, February 21, 1963, p. 1.

"House Bill HR 8171, by Mr. Rogers of Texas." 1963. *Union Calendar* no. 421, pp. 7–11.

U.S. House of Representatives, 88th Congress, Report no. 1010. 1963. Mr. Rogers of Texas, from the Committee on Interior and Insular Affairs, December 9, 1963 – Committed to the Committee of the Whole House on the State of the Union (and ordered to be printed), pp. 1–16.

Talbott, Allen D. 1964. Secretary-Treasurer of the Board of Commissioners of the Third Division Irrigation District. September 17 and November 6.

Jones, Irene. 1976. *Pavillion City*. Published by Irene Jones.

Midvale Irrigation District, editor. 2002. *The History*. Adapted from Bureau of Reclamation files. http://midvaleirrigation.net/History.aspx.

CPSIA information can be obtained
at www.ICGtesting.com
Printed in the USA
LVHW101619060922
727703LV00005B/108